REACHING

THROUGH

TIME

Lurlene McDaniel

REACHING
THROUGH
TIME

THREE NOVELLAS

What's Happened to Me?
When the Clock Chimes
The Mysteries of Chance

DELACORTE PRESS

Text copyright © 2011 by Lurlene McDaniel
Jacket photograph © by Image Source/Getty Images

Visit us on the Web! www.randomhouse.com/teens
Educators and librarians, for a variety of teaching tools,
visit us at www.randomhouse.com/teachers

Library of Congress Cataloging-in-Publication Data
McDaniel, Lurlene.
Reaching through time: three novellas/Lurlene McDaniel.—1st ed.
v. cm.
Summary: Three tales of teenagers experiencing the inexplicable.
Contents: What's happened to me?—When the clock chimes—The mysteries of chance.
ISBN 978-0-385-73461-5 (hardcover trade: alk. paper) — ISBN 978-0-385-90460-5 (library binding: alk. paper) — ISBN 978-0-375-89949-2 (ebook) 1. Children's stories, American. [1. Supernatural—Fiction. 2. Short stories.] I. Title.
PZ7.M4784172Re 2011   [Fic]—dc22   2010020745

The text of this book is set in 14-point Perpetua.
Book design by Vikki Sheatsley
Printed in the United States of America
10 9 8 7 6 5 4 3 2 1
First Edition

CONTENTS

To Josiah, Jedi, Abbie, Olivia,
Kiley, Trevor, Conner and
Gavin—my beloved ones!

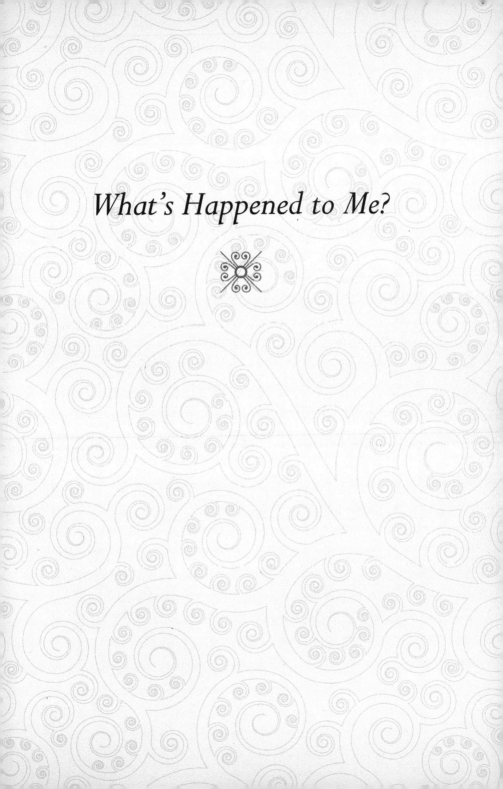

What's Happened to Me?

Beautiful dreamer, wake unto me,
Starlight and dewdrops are waiting for thee;
Sounds of the rude world, heard in the day,
Lull'd by the moonlight have all pass'd away!

—STEPHEN FOSTER (1826–1864)

1

She awoke in the dark, too terrified to move. Her eyes were wide open, but she saw nothing but blackness. Pressure squeezed her chest and she couldn't breathe. She grew light-headed, and just when she thought she would suffocate, she heaved a great gasping breath, like a drowning person breaking the surface of water. Air poured into her lungs and she gagged with the need for it.

At once the darkness was broken by the flare of a single light. "Don't be afraid," a man's voice said in her ear. "I'm right here."

She turned her head to see a glowing candle held aloft, and behind it, his face. Dark hair framed pale skin. He had angular cheekbones and a chiseled jaw, and his eyes were the color of rain. "Who—" she whispered, terror tracing the word.

"Don't be frightened. You're safe. I'm watching over you."

He reached out and stroked her cheek. His touch was cool, soothing, and her brain grew sluggish. She wondered if she had a fever.

"But where—" she asked.

"Time for questions and answers tomorrow," he interrupted. "For now, just sleep."

Her eyelids grew heavy, and despite all her fears, she closed her eyes and obeyed him.

When next she awoke, gray gloom had replaced the dark. She blinked up at a high canopy stretching above the bed where she lay. Tall windows dominated the wall directly in front of the bed, and lead-colored daylight seeped between partially drawn thick velvet drapes. Her heart pounded. She remembered the lighted candle, though, and the voice and face from behind it. She cut her eyes to the bedside.

The young man had kept his promise. He was stretched out in a chair, asleep. In the murky light she saw that her first impression of him had been accurate—dark tendrils of black hair fell over his forehead, and his skin was indeed pale. His hands were draped over the chair's arms, and his fingers were long and tapered, pale and smooth. The other thing she noticed was that he was quite elegant. He was lean, and dressed in leather breeches and a soft, loose white shirt open at his throat.

With one look at him she knew much more about him than she did about herself. Where was she? Who was she?

Why had she no memory of herself? How could a person forget who she was? Her own name? Where memories should have been, she found only black holes.

"You're awake."

His voice startled her. She struggled to sit upright.

He moved quickly and gracefully to sit on the bedding beside her. "No, lie back. You're weak. Let me bring you something to eat."

She was weak. One more thing she didn't understand. He eased her against the pillow. "I'll be right back."

She grasped at his arm. "Please. Tell me what's happened to me."

His eyes, the irises so pale, the pupils black and fathomless, settled on hers. "I'll tell you everything I know as soon as you eat."

He left through a tall wooden door, and the second it closed, she eased to a sitting position. The room spun. She took deep breaths until her vision cleared. She examined the room, saw elaborate tapestries hanging along the wall that butted into the wall of windows and velvet curtains, and another wall heavy with elaborately carved pieces of furniture. Nothing looked familiar, only foreign and foreboding. She closed her eyes, dug deep, searching for some memory, anything that she could hold on to, to tell her about herself and where she was.

She moved her arms and then her legs beneath the covers. Her body worked. Nothing hurt. But her memory was a blank slate. She lifted the covers and saw that she wore a thick white cotton nightgown. Beneath that, she was naked. Before she even had time to wonder about it, the door opened and her benefactor came in carrying a tray. "Here you go—tea and wheat toast with honey. Cream and sugar for your tea."

She pulled the covers up to her chin, fisting the sheets and thick coverlet snugly to her body. "I don't know if I drink tea," she said.

"You'll like it," he said.

He set the tray across her lap and poured steaming brown liquid from a sparkling silver pot into a rose-patterned china cup so thin and finely made she could see through it. He settled himself on her bed to face her. "A little cream, and how about two sugars?"

She watched him drop two small white cubes into the cup with little silver tongs, then pour white cream from a silver pitcher that matched the teapot. He stirred the mixture with a silver spoon and lifted the cup and saucer toward her. "Drink up."

Her hands trembled as she reached for the cup, not wanting to look at him, but unable to help it; her gaze was drawn to his like a magnet to steel. His deep-set eyes were now the color of smoke, the pupils as dark as before. Her heart beat uncontrollably. He smiled warmly and she raised the cup to her mouth. The liquid tasted warm and sweet and began to revive her.

"It's good," she said, prying her gaze away from his.

"Excellent." He grinned, took the cup and picked up the toast and ladled thick golden honey over it.

She took it, ate it. "This is good too."

He leaned back, braced a booted foot against the bedside chair. "Now, as promised, your questions."

She had a million questions, but decided not to let him know she remembered nothing of who she was first thing out of her mouth. "H-how did I end up here?"

"I found you."

"Found me?"

"On my father's estate, up by the entrance gate, just inside. You were lying in a heap on the ground, unconscious."

"But how did I get there?"

He shrugged broad but graceful shoulders. "That I don't know. I was out riding. My horse drew up or he would have stepped on you."

"When was this?"

"A few days ago."

"Days!" She sat up straighter and the tray would have slid away if he hadn't caught it.

"I brought you here," he said, setting the tray on the nearby chair. "To this room. To this bed."

She remembered the gown she was wearing. And what she wasn't wearing under it. "Who dressed me?" She couldn't bring herself to ask "Who undressed me?"

"I did," he said.

Her face burned hot, and she wanted to hide under the thick covers. "Where are my clothes?"

"I burned them."

Her embarrassment turned to shock, then to anger. "You burned them! They might have held a clue about me."

"Your clothing was dirty and torn. I'll find something for you to wear."

"I don't want your clothes. I want mine. I want to go——" She halted. Go where?

He rose from the bed, bowed and gestured toward the door. "You may leave at any time. You're not a prisoner, just a lost girl I rescued from the cold and brought into my home."

Her anger fizzled. "I——I don't mean to be ungrateful. I know you've helped me. It's just that——that . . ." She couldn't finish.

He moved closer to the bed, lifted her chin. Once again, she found his touch cool, as if his hand had been in cold air. "I get that you're frightened. But now that you are here, you're my guest, and you're safe."

She stared up into his compelling eyes. "You don't understand," she whispered, struggling to find words she didn't want to say.

"Tell me."

He might think her insane, but she decided to risk it. "I——I don't know who I am. I have no memory of anything that happened before I woke up in this bed last

night. Nothing. Zero. I don't even know my own name.
Who can't remember their own name?"

He lifted a bit of hair that had fallen across her face
and smoothed it off her forehead, his eyes ever holding
hers. "A person who's struck her head and has tempo-
rary amnesia. You've lost your memory. I'm sure that with
rest it will return. Until then, you're welcome to stay
here and recover. All right?"

Lost. Yes, she was lost in a place she didn't know, with
a stranger she found exciting and mysterious and oddly
disturbing. "What now?" she asked.

"Get your strength back and let me be your friend."
He stepped away, and she was torn between wanting him
to stay and wanting him to leave. He went to the door.

"Wait," she called. "Who are you? I don't know your
name, and you've helped me."

"My bad manners," he said, bowing. "I am Heath de
Charon. Your host."

2

After Heath had shut her door, she swung her legs to the floor. She felt woozy, but once the feeling passed she began to explore her space. The room was large, with ceilings that soared upward, high enough to make the huge canopied bed seem perfectly sized for the space. The stone floor was covered in thick woven rugs, but still the air was chilly and so were her bare feet. She crossed to the windows and tugged on the rich purple drapery, sliding the panels aside to reveal wavy panes of glass and a view of thick gray mist, too thick to see through.

She made her way around the room, touching massive pieces of carved furniture, opening drawers, in which she found a couple of sweaters and not much else. She stopped at a tall piece of furniture with doors and metal handles. She pulled open the doors and discovered a few pairs of slacks and plain white tops along with a long gray dress. Were these the clothes Heath had meant she could wear? She looked down at the simple cotton nightgown, felt another rush of embarrassment. Nothing looked or felt familiar, and she grew irritated all over again. How could Heath have burned her clothes? She wanted to cover herself from head to toe, so she grabbed the long gray dress with its high neck and long sleeves, then rummaged through all the dresser drawers until she discovered a long slip, smooth and soft to her touch. She dressed, hoping both would fit. She shouldn't have wondered—both pieces fit as though they'd been made for her tall lean body.

She found heavy woolen stockings and tugged them on, and beneath a stack of shawls she found a mirror lying facedown. She chewed her bottom lip, hesitant to turn it over, not sure she wanted to look at herself. What would the mirror tell her? Her hand trembled as she turned the mirror upward. What she saw was a girl equal in age to Heath de Charon, with wavy shoulder-length brown hair and blue eyes. What she didn't see was someone she recognized.

"Are you feeling better?" Heath looked up from where he was seated at a gold-ornamented desk when she stepped into the room.

"The toast and tea helped," she said. She'd left her room and crept down wide carpeted stairs lined with a banister of rich dark twisting wood. At the foot of the stairs, a marble floor spread in all directions to thresholds of tall doorways leading to several rooms. She'd discovered Heath behind this desk in one of the rooms.

He rose, smiled and walked to her. "Welcome to the library. I'm catching up on some estate bookkeeping business for my father."

She saw grand shelves that reached to the room's ceiling, every one filled with leather-bound books. Two tall windows allowed gray morning light to fill the room. "I don't want to bother you."

He took her hand and led her to a sofa of soft supple leather. "No trouble." He guided her to sit and he sat beside her, turning in her direction. "I see you found the closet."

Her face went hot as she thought about him undressing her, about his pale eyes seeing her breasts, her curves and intimate mounds. She averted her eyes. "Yes. Thank you."

"I'm sorry you didn't have much of a selection."

"I liked the dress best," she said. "Without my other clothes, I had no idea what to put on."

"You look good in anything. Or in nothing," he added. She felt her face burning.

"I'm embarrassing you. Forgive me." He stood and walked over to his desk. "Please, look around. This won't take much longer."

Anxious to have something to do, she began to make her way around the library, reaching to run her hand along the spines of the many books on one shelf. "You've got a large collection."

"A family obsession."

"Some look really old."

"Most are. It's my job to see they're preserved. Original printings of rare books are also pretty valuable, but that's not why I do it."

She stopped in front of one of the long casement windows, stared out at the thick mist broken only by the top of a hedge that hugged the lowest pane of glass. She wrapped her arms around herself, shivered and fought an urge to cry.

He was next to her in seconds, cupping her chin and raising her face to his. "Don't be afraid. You're safe here."

Tears welled in her eyes and his face blurred. "Why can't I remember anything about myself? I look around and every object has a name. I know what each thing in the room is called. Everything except me. I found a mirror in my room, but I didn't know the face that looked back at me."

"Your memory will return," he assured her.

"What if it doesn't? Are you a doctor?"

"No, but I read all I could find about amnesia."

"Did a doctor—?" She couldn't finish her question because he had laid a finger against her lips.

"Shhh. You're getting worked up and it won't help you remember. The best treatment is to adopt a daily routine and let your memory catch up with you. According to what I've read, when you least expect it, a fragment will return. That will lead you to additional fragments until all your memories come back."

The coolness of his long fingers, the smoothness of his words and the beguiling depths of his eyes calmed her. She decided she must trust him because she had no other choice. "All right," she said softly.

A smile lit the angular planes of his face, making her knees weaken. "Good! Now make yourself comfortable. My home is yours."

She glanced at the books. "I guess I could read." She looked up at him quickly. "Can people with amnesia read? Do we remember how?"

He shrugged. "Perhaps."

She went to a nearby shelf and pulled out a book. She flipped it open, but the words were a jumble of letters. She tried another book. It too was a mass of tangled letters she couldn't decipher. Tears of disappointment filled her eyes. "I—I can't."

Heath took the book from her hands and laid it on the shelf. "Most of my books are in Latin," he said kindly. "A dead language."

"You read in Latin?" She wasn't sure whether to be relieved or embarrassed because she knew nothing about Latin. "Why?"

"A family tradition. My father insisted that I have a

classical education. This way I can go into medicine or law or teaching with a giant head start."

"No books in English?"

"No English, but some are in French." He walked to the other side of the room, pulled three volumes out of the case and brought them to her.

She eagerly flipped open the top one. She couldn't read it. She returned it to him. "No French."

He looked sorry for her. "Don't be sad. I'll keep you busy."

A chill ran through her. How else could she learn about the world? If she couldn't read, what was there to jog any memories locked inside her head?

As if hearing her thoughts, he said, "I'll be your guide. My house, my grounds, my time are devoted to you. Surely over time something of your past will come to you—first a trickle and then a flood."

More than anything she longed to believe him.

"Now," he said, taking her arm and hooking it through his. "It's time for lunch. The dining hall is this way."

She went, not because she was hungry, but because she had nowhere else to go and no one else to lean on except Heath, a boy-man, so totally in control of his world and now hers that she had no choice but to follow him.

3

H e led her out of the library, across the marble floor and into a room with an impossibly long table with rows of chairs on either side. The table was set with pewter plates, ornate silverware, glass goblets and soaring candelabras. She stopped short. "Expecting company?"

He laughed. "This is the banquet hall, but we won't be eating in here. We'll walk through it to get to the morning room."

He led her through another doorway and into a much smaller room with leaded-glass casement windows on three sides. The table was set for two and topped with dome-covered platters. He pulled out a chair. She sat and he took the chair directly across from hers.

"I hope you'll like the food." He lifted a dome and revealed a neatly sliced ham. Other platters held roast potatoes, cooked cabbage and carrots.

Oddly, she knew the names of the foods, and a tingle

on her taste buds let her know she had eaten them before. Or foods like them. "Looks yummy," she said, surprised by the uptick in her appetite. "I think I like ham and potatoes."

He spooned some roasted vegetables onto her plate. "A memory?"

She wasn't sure. "The food just seems familiar. That's all."

"See? I told you that your memory would return gradually."

"I'd rather know my name," she said, slicing some ham and tasting it.

"We could give you a name."

"No," she said quickly. "I want to remember on my own. Everyone has a name."

"I'm sure yours will fit you perfectly."

She heard an intimate tone in his words, but didn't meet his gaze, looking instead over his head and out the window into the swirling mist. "Is the weather always like this? Does the sun ever shine?"

"You've arrived during a dark part of the year, but yes, the sun will shine again."

"And you'll show me all around when the sun comes out?"

"If you like."

She ate her food, listening to the clank of the silver against the fine china plates. Heath wasn't eating much, only gazing from her to a window. She became self-conscious and slowed her eating. She searched for something to say to him, something neutral that would shift the topic of conversation from her. "When will I meet your father?"

Heath looked at her blankly.

"You told me this was your father's estate."

Heath straightened. "He's away on business. I never know when he'll return."

"So are you by yourself?"

"Usually."

"No mother? Brothers, sisters?"

"Only me."

"Well, who takes care of this place? It seems huge."

"I have help."

She looked around, listened carefully for sounds of life from any direction. "Who?"

"They come and go. It isn't their habit to be seen."

This sounded creepy to her. She also realized that without others in the great house, she was alone with him. She cleared her throat. "I guess it makes sense that this food doesn't appear by magic."

"It appears. That's all that matters to us."

Her stomach tightened. He'd said "us." What did he mean? "I don't belong here," she told him. "I came from . . . well, from someplace else."

"Of course, you're right. This is my world, not yours." He stood abruptly. "I still have some work to do."

She pushed her plate away, her appetite gone.

"You can finish your lunch."

"I'm full."

He studied her. "I shouldn't be too long. Feel free to explore. Come get me if you're bored."

She experienced again the feeling of wanting him to leave and wanting him to stay. "I'll just poke around."

He tipped his head and left the morning room.

She sat at the table listening to the silence. The place was eerie and made her feel confined despite its spaciousness. Finally she arose, walked back through the banquet room and out into the hallway. From there she turned into another room filled with tapestries, large sofas and slouchy chairs, and on one wall, a fireplace so massive that it took her breath away.

She approached the hearth made of blackened brick and laid with fresh logs waiting for kindling and a match. She stepped up on the raised hearth, but although she stood on tiptoe, her fingertips could only brush the bottom of the stone mantel. She moved to one side to examine one of the posts holding up the great mantel. They too were made of stone, and chiseled so elaborately that it took her a few minutes to figure out what she was seeing. On the right-hand side, from top to bottom there were figures of winged creatures hovering above people toiling over crops or harvesting sheaves of wheat, of men in fishing boats and of men in armor on horses, carrying

waving banners. Every inch of the old stone post was covered with carvings.

She crossed to the left side of the mantel and saw carvings of mythical creatures, most fearsome and hideous:
wolfmen, vampires, flying bats and gargoyles. She shivered. And yet she recognized the carved images as mon-
sters and demons by name. Why? How could she know
what they were but not be able to name herself?

"I'm sorry. I shouldn't have left you." Heath's voice
from behind startled her so much that she fell backward
off the hearth. With lightning speed, he was there to catch
her and stand her upright.

"Y-you scared me!" she cried.

"Then I owe you another apology. I'm sorry for scaring you."

She twisted in his hold and glanced into his face, which
now looked boyish and ashamed. His irises were as clear
as water. "I understood that you have work to do."

"I have nothing to do that's more important than making you feel comfortable. I know that you're lost and confused. Perhaps my world seems strange to you."

An understatement, she thought, but didn't say it
aloud. "Your home is amazing," she said. "Like this fireplace." She touched one of the cold stone carvings. "So
lifelike."

"Always been one of my favorites. I used to sit and
study it for hours, seeing something different every time
I did. It was created for the estate over many years by the

same family of stonecutters. It represents the work of many hands."

"Why are the two sides so different?"

"One side represents the spirituality of mankind; the other, his mythology and stories. Both sides make up the human spirit. At least, that's the family lore. I think it was just a way for the stonecutters to stay busy for a few hundred years." He smiled, mischief in his expression.

She studied the spiritual side more closely and saw the Star of David beneath the feet of one winged being, and a many-armed god that sat cross-legged beneath the feet of another. "It's very beautiful," she said.

"I love beautiful things."

She felt heat rise in her neck.

He took her hand. "Come on. Let me show you around. You've barely seen my home."

"You mean your castle."

A smile flirted with the corners of his sensual mouth. "It's called the Chateau de Charon."

"How old is it?"

"Parts of it were begun in the twelfth century. It was modernized somewhat—you know, indoor plumbing and heating. Inefficient heating, I'm afraid. No electricity, though. A few ancestors thought that too modern for its history."

"And after my tour?"

"Dinner and sleep."

"Didn't we just eat lunch?"

"We ate more than three hours ago."

Her mouth dropped open. "But—but—I haven't been in this room more than a few minutes."

He helped her off the hearth. "Not really. You've been in here for several hours. I've been working and feeling guilty about leaving you alone."

She shook her head as if to unstick something. She was certain he was wrong. Only minutes had passed since lunch. And yet she was growing hungry. Could he be correct? Had hours passed with her totally unaware of it?

"Come," he said, clasping her hand. "Time can sneak up on you in this place. We'll sit together in the library. I have a fire going in there."

She went without a word, afraid that time would again get away from her. So long as she was with him, she had an anchor. She needed an anchor in this mysterious place.

They spent the afternoon, or what seemed like an afternoon to her, in the library in front of a roaring fire that took the chill off the room. He read. She sat almost as if in a trance, staring at the flames. At some point Heath announced that dinner was ready—she hadn't heard anyone come into the room with the news, but she went with him. They ate together, still with only each other and no other people. The food was perfectly prepared and utterly delicious. Heath tried to lighten her mood, but she was sad and couldn't make herself feel cheerful. Too many unanswered questions. Too many unexplainable things on her mind.

When Heath said goodnight, he walked her up the staircase, handed her a candle. "Your bed's turned down and your fireplace lit," he said.

When? Who? "Thanks," she said.

"I promise tomorrow will be better," he said softly. His eyes were like pools of liquid silver and totally mesmerizing.

She struggled to break their hold on her. "And sunny?"

"And sunny."

She clutched the candle, hurried into the bedroom, her heart pounding and her breath rapid. She set down the candle, saw that the room was bathed in the glow of a blaze in the fireplace. A soft white nightgown lay across the bed for her. Her hands shook as she removed the dress and put on the gown. A lump clogged her throat and she wanted to cry.

Cry for what? she asked herself. I'm safe. She blew out the candle and climbed under the fresh rose-scented covers. Her eyelids grew heavy, as if weights had been placed on them.

She felt herself drifting toward sleep, was almost asleep . . . when soft whispering voices emerged from the shadows, calling, "Sarah . . . Sarah . . . come back to me. . . . I love you."

4

"My name is Sarah." She made the announcement as she walked into the morning room, where Heath was already seated at the table.

His eyes, pale gray in the light, bore into hers. "How do you know that?"

She hesitated to tell him about the whispering voices she'd heard throughout the night, though she wasn't sure why—Heath was trying to help her. Still, she held back the information. The first mysterious voice had been joined by others: a man, a woman, a buzz of words that seemed to float in and hover above her bed. The voices had said the name too many times for her to believe that it wasn't hers. They had soothed and comforted her, like salve on the wound of her lost memory. "I—I just know."

Heath's smile broke across his handsome face. "Good. Then I'll call you Sarah." He stood, pulled out her chair. "Eat breakfast with me."

Sarah sat, feeling relieved to finally have put a name to her face.

"Look," he said, gesturing to the windows.

The glass was opaque, but she saw brightness through the panes. "Sunshine?"

"As promised." He tipped his head at her.

Her heart leapt. "We can go outside?"

"We'll go riding."

"Riding? In what?"

He laughed. "On horses."

"I—I don't think . . . I mean, I don't know if I can ride a horse." Her memory circuits shut down, and the thrill she'd felt over learning her name faded.

"You'll be able to ride," Heath said. "Trust me."

What choice did she have? She couldn't stand the idea of being cooped up one more minute. "All right." She looked down at the gray dress she was wearing, the same one as yesterday. "I don't think I can ride in this."

"After breakfast go up and change. I'll meet you at the foot of the stairs."

She hurried through the meal, bounded up the staircase. In her room, she threw open the doors of the wardrobe and blinked. Every item from the day before was gone, and in its place were jeans, T-shirts, turtleneck sweaters and fleece jackets. Her skin went cold. When had the clothing been changed out? Had someone come into her room while she slept? Maybe while she was at breakfast . . .

Ignoring her internal questions, she grabbed jeans, a tee and a jacket, threw off the dress and tugged on the new clothes. Immediately she felt a kind of familiarity about the perfectly fitting outfit. She found boots that also fit at the bottom of the wardrobe. She bounded back downstairs, where Heath waited.

He eyed her head to toe in a way that made her heart thud. Such compelling eyes. "Ready?" he asked.

They went outside and into a world of rolling green lawn, clipped hedges and flower beds that stretched as far as Sarah could see. She stopped short and blinked against the brightness of the sun. "Wow. It's beautiful out here."

"I'm glad you think so."

"Where to now?"

"Up for a walk to the stables?"

She couldn't wait to walk in the warm sunlight.

They took a footpath that wound down a hillside toward a building in the distance. Her gaze darted every which way, taking in the extraordinary beauty of the grounds. "Where are we?" she asked.

"At my family estate," he reminded her.

"Yes, but where? What country? If I know, maybe it will jog a memory."

"My country is unimportant."

"Does your family own a country too?" she asked, irritated. She was bothered by his information hoarding. Didn't he realize that every clue was important to her?

"I'm not trying to annoy you. It's important that you recover memories on your own."

"Is that something you read in one of your moldy books in Latin about amnesia?"

He stopped and turned her to face him. His black hair spilled over his pale forehead, and his eyes darkened. For a moment she regretted her sarcasm. "You remembered your name. You're sure of it. Go slowly." His voice was soft, beguiling.

Looking into his eyes made her feel spellbound. "I didn't mean to sound ungrateful," she said.

He grinned, leaned forward and kissed her forehead. His lips were cool, but the spot where they had pressed her skin felt hot. Deep in her memory, the shadow of another's kiss darted just out of reach. Warm lips on hers. A pang of longing shot through her for—

"You all right?" he asked, looking concerned.

"Fine," she lied. "Can we get to the stables? I'd love that tour you promised."

He stepped back, his expression intense. "Come with me."

The stable was clean and sweet-smelling, heavy with the scent of fresh straw and horseflesh. At one stall a great gray horse stuck his head over the door and neighed at the sight of Heath. He reached up and rubbed the horse's nose.

"Titan, meet our guest," Heath said to the horse, which blew out through his nostrils and shook his head.

Sarah laughed. "Hello, Titan."

Heath led Titan from his stall and walked to another. "This one's yours." He opened the door and ushered out a smaller red roan with a thick black mane. "Lethe," Heath said. "One of my finest mares. Gentle as a kitten. No need to be afraid of her."

Sarah had drawn back. Her blank memory held no information about horses.

In minutes, Heath had both horses saddled and bridled. He cupped his hands and urged Sarah to step into them. "I'll give you a leg up."

Sarah hesitated, but then stepped into Heath's hands and swung her leg over the back of the red horse. The second she settled into the saddle, she felt as if she were one with Lethe. Why couldn't she recall ever riding before? Being in the saddle felt natural to her.

They left the barn, riding out into the sunlight. "I know where I want to go," Sarah said. "Please take me to the place where you found me unconscious."

Heath said, "There's nothing to see."

"Please."

They rode silently over rolling land until the ground grew rocky and the grass sparse and brown. The sun went behind clouds; a cool breeze ruffled Sarah's hair and Lethe's mane. At last Sarah saw a black iron fence in the distance with a large double gate. They went closer and she saw that the fence was quite high, with evenly spaced bars that came to sharp points at the top. Mist and gloom rolled just outside the fence. Lethe pranced sideways, straining against her bridle as they approached. "How come it's so foggy on the other side?"

"Sometimes the fog hangs around for hours," Heath said. "Just the climate around here."

"What's on the other side of your property?" Sarah asked. Lethe neighed nervously.

"Unfriendly neighbors."

Sarah was shocked. "Like who?"

"People who want to steal our property. Sometimes they stand at the fence for hours and howl like wolves."

The hair on her arms rose and the back of her neck tingled. She imagined an angry mob reaching through the fence bars. "Are you in danger?"

"This fence goes into a stone wall that surrounds my family's estate. It's high and impregnable. No one can get in."

Sarah squinted into the gloom, but could see nothing beyond the fence barrier. She was also feeling anxious, as if the fog wasn't friendly. "Where did you find me?"

"Over here, by the gate," Heath said.

She urged Lethe toward the gate, but the animal shied away. Heath spoke to Lethe and she calmed, walked to the gate, where Sarah stared down at the hard rock-strewn ground. She saw no clues, no hint about her identity, and couldn't imagine how she had ever ended up there. "Is the gate locked?"

"Always."

"But how——?"

"A mystery," Heath said, coming alongside her. "Accept that you just came to be here and that now you're safe."

Perhaps it was the gloom, but when Sarah looked into his face she saw that his pale gray eyes had darkened. It was difficult for her to accept his explanation the way he wanted her to. She had come from somewhere, but where? And how had she breached the impregnable gates?

"Come back," he said. "Let me show you the gardens, the creek and the woods."

She nodded, unwilling to press an argument with him. She would have to figure it out on her own. Maybe the voices would return that night and tell her something. As they rode away from the gate, Sarah glanced back one time only to see the fence holding back the soupy mist like a wall. It looked freaky, and she wondered—if nothing could get in, did that also mean nothing could get out?

As they rode back over the grounds, Sarah noted that the sun was setting and long shadows were being cast on the rolling grass. "Is it late?" she asked above the sound of the horses' hooves.

"Night's coming," Heath said.

"Are you serious? We just got outside."

"No. We've been out here for hours."

"No way." She felt profound disappointment. To her, it seemed that almost no time had passed since they'd left the stables.

"Look at the lather on our horses' necks. They're tired and want to return to the stables."

Heath was right. Lethe's neck was sweaty.

Sarah felt a twinge of guilt. She hadn't meant to push the horse hard, but she couldn't get over the feeling that little time had passed since they'd saddled up.

At the stable she and Heath dismounted and Heath said, "Let's walk back to the house while we still have light."

"But the horses—don't you have to take off their saddles and put them back in their stalls?"

"They'll be fed and watered, then groomed and put away."

She craned her neck, searching for any other people, but saw no one. "Are your grooms invisible?"

"No, just busy with other things." Heath slipped his hand over Sarah's, his touch cool and firm. "Time for dinner. I'm hungry."

Sarah felt as if they'd just eaten breakfast, but her stomach growled in anticipation. She found Heath's world both strange and enticing. Of course, she had no memory of her own time and place, so how could she criticize his? One thing was certain, though—his world had an amazing way of measuring time.

5

Sarah awoke in the dark, her heart hammering like a drum. A whispering voice was calling to her. "Sarah . . . Sarah . . . I love you. Come back. . . ." She sat upright in the bed. The room was wrapped in darkness. The fireplace, stacked with burning logs when she'd gone to bed, was now cold. She scooted from under the warm covers and, shivering, wrapped herself in a heavy coverlet and edged her way around the room's perimeter. "Who are you?" she whispered to the walls. "Where are you?"

A male voice said, "If you can hear me, baby, take my hand." His voice sounded hauntingly familiar.

She reached into the void but could feel nothing. "I'm right here," she said.

"They say you might be able to hear me, so I'm going to keep talking to you."

"I can hear you!"

"Your mom and dad are at dinner, so it's just me and you now," he said.

Parents? Why couldn't she remember them? "Who are you?" she called out. Her voice reverberated in the silence of the room. She clamped a hand across her mouth. She should keep her voice down. What if she woke Heath?

The male voice said, "Remember when we met? I plowed into you in the hall and knocked you flat. I felt like an idiot. You were so pretty and I was a klutz—and still am. You could have yelled at me, but you laughed and made me feel like it was your fault too. But it wasn't."

Her head was beginning to hurt from the strain of trying to remember. The voice was soft and comforting. She wanted to go into it so much. "I—I don't remember . . . ," she whispered, brokenhearted.

"Then when we found ourselves sitting next to each other in Chem One, I told myself, 'Justin, you lucked out. Don't mess this up by saying something stupid.'"

Justin. Sarah had another name. She tried to find a face to put with it, but the strain was too much. "I want to remember! I—I can't . . . ," she said to the darkness.

"Your friends call every day asking about you. I tell them nothing's changed. I won't give up, Sarah. None of us will. I love you."

The voice receded and she was again alone and feeling lost. She made her way to the window, pushed against the glass. It was hard and unyielding beneath her palms. The voice, this Justin, must be a hallucination, her imagination gone wild in the night. She recalled no family, no friends, no Justin who said he loved her. She crumpled to the floor and wept.

"You look tired," Heath said as they walked to the stables after breakfast. "Aren't you sleeping well?"

A golden sun shone down from a cerulean sky and warmed Sarah's head and shoulders. "I had a strange dream and couldn't get back to sleep," she said.

He stopped. "A dream? Are you sure?"

She didn't want to tell him, "Actually, I'm probably going crazy—I hear voices all night long." Instead, she waved her hand dismissively. "Just a weird dream. No biggie."

"People don't usually dream when they're here."

She puzzled over his statement. "Why wouldn't some-one dream when they're here?"

His eyes, so pale moments before, darkened. "It's the air, I think. Very pure, so sleep is pure too."

She tried to recall whether she'd had other dreams during her nights on his estate, but couldn't. He touched her forehead, and whatever questions she had grew fuzzy. What had she and Heath been discussing? She shook her head to clear it.

Heath had quickly moved ahead of her on the path to the stable, and she had to jog to catch up to him. He led the horses out of their stalls, saddled both and helped her mount Lethe. "I want to show you the grounds."

They rode in silence, the horses prancing and straining at their bits. Heath's horse, Titan, seemed especially
ready to run. But Sarah was in no hurry. The strangeness
of the night before had faded and she felt content in the
sun and air and with Heath's company. Again she struggled to remember what they'd been talking about minutes
before. It had been important to her, but now, under the
lulling sun and sky, with the horse moving and the rhyth-
mic sound of hooves hitting the ground, Sarah couldn't
dredge up what the conversation had been about.

They crested a hill and Heath reined in Titan. "Look,"
he said.

Below, Sarah saw gardens with fields of flowers. The
beauty took her breath away.

Heath said, "Let's walk. The horses can graze."

He dismounted, came to her and reached up. She
swung her leg over the back of her horse and he grasped
her waist. His hands tightened as he lowered her. She slid
slowly down the length of his hard muscled body, her
pulse throbbing and her heart thudding. He pressed
against her. Caught between him and the horse, Sarah had
neither will nor desire to move aside. His eyes, riveted on
hers, were clear as water, the pupils small and jet-black.
She felt as if she might drown in those eyes.

"Touch me," he whispered.

Slowly she raised her arms to settle them around his
neck. With one hand she toyed with the curls at the nape
of his neck, then smoothed the curls spilling across his

forehead. Soft as silk . . . His skin was pale and smooth and cool in spite of the sun's heat. Time stood still.

Behind her, Lethe shifted, ambled off to graze near Titan. In that moment, Sarah gasped like a swimmer coming up for air, breaking the spell and Heath's hold on her waist. Flustered, she said, "W-we should walk."

Heath's eyes darkened slightly, but he grinned and said, "All right."

Her legs were rubbery, but she headed down the hill toward the blooming gardens. Footpaths meandered every which way beside flower beds, each bed more gorgeous than the one before. When they came to endless beds of roses, Sarah stopped. Each rose looked luminescent in the sunlight, every bush full and every flower perfect. Colors of every shade and hue stretched as far as she could see. The heady perfumed air made her dizzy.

"You like?" Heath asked.

"They're so beautiful. I—I don't know what to say."

"Some of these bushes have been here a hundred years," he said.

"Are you kidding? That's so long. Who takes care of them?"

"We have gardeners whose only job is to keep the flowers and trees healthy."

Sarah turned in a circle, searching for the gardeners who kept such perfect roses. "Where are they?"

"They come in the early morning and the evening. Too hot in the middle of the day," Heath said.

"You know, I've been here for days and I've never seen any other people." She started walking along the paths between the beds as she spoke.

"Is that so bad? To only be with me?" Heath kept step beside her.

"Of course not. I just think it would be nice to talk to other people. Maybe someone might have a clue about me—who I am or where I came from."

"You're Sarah and you came from outside," Heath said. "It was the happiest day of my life when I found you."

His words made her pause. Finally she said, "I'm not complaining . . . just wondering. When I try and remember stuff about myself, my head hurts and I get sad."

"Sarah, what does the past matter? You're here now with me."

"But you know who you are. You're proud of your home and your past. I hear it in your voice when you talk about it."

He pulled her closer. Lifting her chin with his forefinger, he said, "I haven't given up searching for your home. I've sent out inquiries, but I just haven't heard anything yet."

"You have?" Her heart leapt. "Why didn't you tell me?"

"I'll tell you when I hear something. If you had known, as you do now, you'd be asking me every day for news. Wouldn't you?" he teased.

He was right about that. "Every other day," she fudged, making him laugh.

She smiled too, and he traced the corner of her lips with his finger. "That's better. You have a pretty smile."

She didn't want to get caught in his gaze again, so she turned and continued down the path. She hadn't gone far when off to one side she saw an enormous hedge of thick bushes, perfectly clipped and maintained, every leaf neat and trimmed. The hedge was easily fifteen feet high. It looked solid, but she spied an opening, a boxlike door cut into the branches. "What's that?" she called to Heath, who had fallen back, letting her go ahead.

"A maze," he said. "But don't—"

Sarah laughed and darted like a rabbit toward the opening. "Catch me!"

She never made it through the hole. Heath seemed to arrive instantly at her side. He seized her elbow and spun her around. "Don't go in there!" he commanded. "Don't ever go in there."

6

Sarah shrank from him, terrified by the look on his face and the steel in his voice. His eyes had turned dark and foreboding, like thunder clouds ready to storm. "You're hurting my arm," she squeaked.

Instantly he let go and closed his eyes. He rocked back on his heels. "I'm sorry. I didn't mean to hurt you. You scared me, that's all."

"How?" She rubbed her elbow.

"I didn't want you to go into the maze." His eyes opened and they were a lighter shade of gray. "It's dangerous."

He reached out to touch her, but she shrugged him off. "Dangerous . . . how?"

"It's a very old maze. See how tall and thick the boxwood are?"

"I see that."

"Many years ago, some ancestor constructed it for

people to play in. A master maze maker was hired to create it in the fourteenth century. He was the best my family's money could buy. The boxwood were shorter then, and you could see over the tops of the bushes. Lots of light came in. Now it's grown too tall and it's dark along the inside paths. The maze is a giant puzzle, almost impossible to navigate and treacherous with dead ends. People have gotten lost in it."

"People get lost in it?" Sarah repeated.

"True story. They can't find their way out and the bushes muffle their cries when we search for them."

"How do you find them?" The idea was frightening. Lost inside a maze like a trapped mouse.

"We only find them when buzzards begin to circle."

She shivered. "Really?"

He nodded. "The very brave tie a rope around their waist and wander through it. We always have to pull them out, though."

"So no one gets out by themselves?"

"Perhaps some have, but not for a long time. It's easier to make it off-limits."

She peered at the opening. It did look dark and unfriendly. "You should put a chain up. And a sign."

Heath nodded. "Yes, we should. I'll speak to the head gardener." He flipped her hair. She didn't draw away this time. "We should be getting back. I'm sure the horses have stuffed their bellies with grass by now. Almost time for supper for us too. Aren't you hungry?"

Supper! Sarah could hardly believe so much time had passed, but she saw long shadows stretching across the path. The hedge maze looked even more ominous in the shadows. "Yes," she answered, thinking that time was an oddity on Heath's estate. It either passed too quickly or stretched beyond belief.

They retraced their steps along the pathway, past beds of flowers growing dim in the gathering darkness. "Why don't you cut it down?" she asked. "The maze, I mean. What good is it if it can hurt people?"

"I've wondered that too. I was told because it's very old. It would be wrong to destroy plants that have weathered several hundred years of survival. So we allow it to stand and grow older and warn visitors away from it."

She didn't say it, but she had plainly seen that the great maze was well cared for. It was groomed and cut and nurtured, and perfectly manicured. Why would gardeners waste their time on keeping up a thing considered so dangerous and deadly?

The voices came at night. Long nights that Sarah lost track of in a jumble of days and riding with Heath. Sarah gave up answering the voices—she couldn't make herself heard—and just lay in the bed listening to them, to the cadences and the sincerity in their tone. She wasn't afraid of hearing them anymore. To the contrary, the voices soothed and comforted her. The one called Mother shared all kinds of stories about family that Sarah wished she could connect to, but no matter how she tried, her memory door was shut and locked. The voice called Dad read to her—charming fairy tales and stories about princesses being rescued by handsome knights. But it was the Justin voice that touched her the most. His voice was soft, gentle. He told her things about a place called school and about people whose names she didn't know. Mostly he told her how he missed her and how much he loved her and how much he wanted to hold her and kiss her and touch her the way he once did. She cried when the voices faded, usually when the sun rose and gleamed through the window of her room on Heath's estate.

Strangely, she was never tired in the mornings, and was always ready to face a day of riding with Heath, of slipping through endless forests, of watching the falcon that Heath had trained to ride on his gloved hand. "Sharp talons," Heath had explained to Sarah. She thought the bird majestic. It wore a leather hood decorated with a single white plume.

Morning followed night, and days melted into one another. On one gleaming morning, Heath reined in Titan on the crest of a hill overlooking an open field. Sarah stopped beside him on Lethe. The sun bounced off the droplets of dew, making it look as if jewels had been sprinkled across the grass. The air smelled sharp and sweet with wildflowers. The feathers of the falcon on Heath's glove shimmered.

Heath stroked the bird and said, "He needs to hunt."

He pulled off the hood and the great bird blinked. Heath held up his arm and the bird took flight.

Sarah watched it soar into the blue sky, circling, spiraling ever higher, until she lost sight of him against the sun. "Will he come back?"

"Always. He was trained on a tether and forgets that he's no longer on it. He'll hunt, eat and return to his roost."

She watched the bird swoop down, disappear into faraway woods. "Does he ever fly over the fence? You know, to the outside?"

"No. He has all that he needs here. He's contented."

Sarah read between the lines. She wasn't contented, and Heath must have sensed it. Like he did with the falcon, Heath gave her all she needed—food, clothing, his company, his undivided attention. So why wasn't she content? She didn't know. The voices made her long for something else, but with no memories beyond waking up at Heath's estate, she had no idea what the "something else" was for her.

She sent a sidelong look at Heath. The breeze ruffled his hair. He had a noble air. He was handsome and self-assured, and he liked her. She was wary of him, though. Beneath his surface lay a dimension she couldn't fathom, a mystery she couldn't touch.

He turned toward her, catching her off guard. "Are you staring at me?"

Embarrassed, she averted her gaze. "I'm not staring."

"Okay. You were looking hard. Have I grown a wart on my face?"

"No warts," she said. Anxious not to be quizzed, she dug her heels into Lethe's side and yelled, "Just wondering if you can keep up."

Lethe bolted away, and in seconds Sarah heard Titan thundering behind her. She laughed, yelled over her shoulder, "Your nag is slow!"

Wind whipped Sarah's hair. She leaned low into the horse's neck and felt the sting of Lethe's flying mane on her cheek. Sun beat on her back, and she felt the flexing muscles of the horse between her legs. Exhilaration shot through her. In minutes she and the horse had crossed the meadow and reached a part of the estate that didn't look familiar. When an iron fence loomed up, Sarah reined Lethe hard to avoid crashing into it. Lethe pulled back and stopped short, throwing Sarah forward and almost over the horse's head. Seconds later, Heath and Titan were by their side.

"You all right?" Heath asked, his amusement at the chase replaced by alarm.

"We could have crashed!" she cried, her pulse pounding from the near disaster. The fence had seemed to appear out of nowhere. Only Lethe's quick action had prevented an accident.

"Lethe wouldn't have let you get hurt."

Still trembling, Sarah looked around. "Where are we?"

"I'll show you." Heath slid off Titan and grabbed

Lethe's reins. "Here's a riddle for you, dear Sarah. What brings equality to all men and women, to royalty and beggars, to rich and poor, to old and young, to friends and foes? Can you tell me?"

Without waiting for him to give her a hand, Sarah dismounted and peered through the solid bars of the low fence. Behind the cold black iron rails lay an ancient cemetery.

7

She knew the answer to his riddle but didn't respond. Heath tied their horses to the fence and took Sarah's hand. "You're shivering."

"I'm okay now." Her heart had slowed as she settled herself.

"This is where my ancestors are buried. Let me show you. Nothing here to be frightened of."

"I'm not scared," she said with more bravado than she felt. She didn't want to wander around burial grounds, yet when they stepped through the gate, her apprehension turned to fascination. She saw great slabs of gray granite, towering monoliths etched with coats of arms, knights brandishing swords, fearsome lions and dreaded gargoyles all frozen in time and guarding the dead. Moss and age had settled on every headstone and monument. Her eyes were drawn to a rearing horse so beautifully chiseled that it looked ready to come to life. "How old is this place?"

"No need to whisper," Heath said. "No one here but the dead, and they can't hear you."

Her face went hot. "Was I whispering?"

He held her hand more tightly. He leaned close to her ear and whispered, "Yes."

She looked and saw that he was grinning. "It doesn't seem respectful to shout," she said with a haughty sniff.

As they walked the area, Sarah caught glimpses of names and dates. Hundreds of years were reflected on the old headstones. "Fourteen hundred and fifty-one," she read off one. "Seventeen hundred and five," she read off another. "And all of these people were members of your family?"

"Everyone buried here has a connection to the de Charon name one way or another."

"Pretty big family," she said, looking out over the haphazard collection of grave markers that stretched as far as she could see.

"We cover the earth," he said in a conspiratorial whisper.

She wondered about her history, her family. Somewhere people wanted her to come to them. They told her so every night. She was deep in thought when Heath stopped in front of a large rectangular building. "What's this?" She inspected the smooth, windowless granite surface, its entrance marked by a massive wooden door.

"It's a mausoleum. I'll show you inside." Heath produced a key, opened the door and walked into a dark hallway. In minutes, he'd lit a row of candles hanging on the walls.

Sarah peeked through the open doorway, unsure she wanted to follow him. The place was spooky and gave her the shivers. Smeared by candle smoke, the air smelled musty and was eerily quiet.

"Come on," he urged. "No one here but the dead."

She wasn't comforted, but she hesitantly stepped onto the narrow marble floor, between two high walls with small brass nameplates running their length in straight lines. Some of the plates had names on them; others were blank.

"For future de Charons," Heath said, coming alongside her and running his fingers over a smooth piece of brass.

"You too?"

"Me too," he said. "And those who come after me."

His breath brushed her cheek. A chill shot up her back. In the flickering candlelight, Heath looked otherworldly, ethereal, capable of melting away like icy mist. His skin was the color of the stone, his eyes, translucent. It was as if he'd stepped off the side of the carved fireplace at his estate. How had she ended up in a graveyard with the person who had become her caretaker?

"What are you thinking, pretty Sarah? Tell me."

"You'll laugh at me."

"I won't laugh. Promise."

"Are you a vampire?"

In spite of his promise, Heath laughed. "There is no such things as vampires. They're myths. Made-up stories."

She felt foolish now that she'd asked such a question, so she tried to make light of it. "So you aren't going to turn me into a creature of the night? Suck my blood and make me sleep in a coffin? Because I'm telling you, this girl won't be sleeping in a dirty coffin."

Heath rocked with laughter. "You have some imagination."

"A girl needs to ask these things," she said with a toss of her head. "Accommodations matter."

"Would a vampire wear this?" Heath sobered, reached inside his shirt, pulled out a gold chain and dangled a thick gold cross in front of her eyes. "It's Byzantine," he said. "One of my ancestors wore it fighting in the Crusades."

She somehow knew that vampires were warded off by crosses—a vexing thought, because she could recall such trivial information but remembered nothing about her own life. She crossed her arms. "Okay, nix the vampire. Are you a werewolf? A goblin? Maybe a troll? Maybe you're a sorcerer? I know—a dragon slayer!"

Still laughing, he grabbed her hand and guided her out of the mausoleum.

Leaving the airless tombs and hearing his laughter buoyed her spirits and vanquished her dark mood.

"All of the above," Heath said when they reached the

horses, where he pulled her close against his body. "I'm just someone who adores you, Sarah. Now mount your horse. I've got a special surprise waiting for you in the woods."

Heath's surprise was a picnic by a stream deep in the forest. A blanket was laid out by the stream's banks, along with a large basket and a magnificent feast. Sarah saw salads, meats, cheeses, thick slices of dark bread, bowls of luscious fruit, delicately frosted cupcakes and a plate of delectable chocolates. Pewter goblets held cold cider. She stared at the bounty of food. "Who else is coming?" she asked.

"It's for us. Just us."

"We'll never eat all this food."

"We can try."

"Well . . . if you insist." She sat on the blanket, tucking her legs under herself.

Heath sat beside her, reached for a strawberry and teased her lips with it.

She grabbed it out of his hand and popped it into her mouth, making him laugh. "When did you do this?" she asked, after swallowing the delectable berry. "We've been together all day."

"I have my ways," he said, his clear eyes sparkling.

She glanced around. Except for the horses grazing on brush, they were alone. "You tell me there are others here, but I never see them. Why don't I ever see anyone else?"

His eyes darkened. "Aren't I enough for you?"

She drew back, not wanting to spoil his good humor. "I just want to say thanks to the people who take care of me. My room's always cleaned, my sheets are fresh, my clothes are washed and put away. I have to see the good guys in order to thank them."

"I'll pass along your good wishes." He leaned back on his elbows.

Sarah plucked a grape from the bowl of fruit and fed it to him. "Well, I like everything on the menu. Can I make you a sandwich?"

"Make yours first."

She bypassed the bread and meat and grabbed a cupcake.

"You can't have dessert before lunch."

"Watch me," she said, popping the petite cupcake into her mouth after licking off the sugary frosting.

"You're so bad."

The food tasted delicious. Sarah savored every bite, aware that she ate more than Heath did. She usually did; he wasn't a big eater. She'd tried to hold herself back in the beginning, but she'd stopped doing that. She was hungry at every meal, so she ate as much as she liked. As for Heath, on this afternoon, he merely propped himself up on an elbow and watched Sarah eat.

When she was sated, she rolled up her jeans and kicked off her riding boots.

"What now?" Heath wanted to know.

"I'm going wading. The water's calling my name—hear it?" She mimicked in a high-pitched voice, "Sarah . . . come cool your tootsies."

"The water's bound to be cold. It comes from the mountains. Your feet will freeze."

"I'm not a wimp. I can take it."

He grinned, lay flat on the blanket and closed his eyes. "Watch your step. The rocks are slippery."

"I'll be careful."

She jogged down the slight embankment and waded into the water tumbling across rocks and tree roots. The stream was liquid ice, and she would have retreated but didn't want to give Heath the satisfaction of being right. In minutes, her feet were numb. Still she walked defiantly downstream.

She hadn't gone too far when she came to a small whirlpool in the middle of the stream where the water swirled clockwise. She bent down, intrigued by the cone-shaped motion. She couldn't see the bottom of the creek bed. What she did see was a boy's face smiling up at her. She almost screamed and jumped back, but the face looked so familiar that she stared and held her breath.

His image was clear as a picture—smiling brown eyes, spiky brown hair, full lips and round dimpled cheeks. Her heart leapt with joy. She reached down to touch the achingly familiar face but only touched cold water. For an instant her blank memory cleared. "Justin!" she whispered. "Justin. Don't leave me!"

8

Sarah heard Heath call her name, turned to see him wading down the stream toward her. She didn't want him to know what she had seen in the whirlpool, didn't want to confess that she remembered the name belonging to the face. She spun, made a production of falling and sat down in the water, forcing a laugh as she landed. "You were right," she yelled to Heath. "I slipped."

He reached down to help her up. "You're soaking wet."

"Just my bottom half." Her teeth chattered as the cold water soaked into her jeans and then her skin.

"Let me help," he said. He scooped her up in his arms.

His strength surprised her. He moved effortlessly, as if she'd been a leaf in the water.

"I—I can walk," she told him.

He ignored her, carried her back over the rocks and up the embankment to the blanket. He rummaged in the picnic basket and dragged out a smaller blanket and wrapped it around her. He pulled her down beside him and rubbed her legs and feet with the rough wool. "It's one of the horses' blankets. I'm sorry, it's all I have."

"I deserve it," she said. "You warned me. My feet went right out from under me."

Heath studied her face, and Sarah was terrified that he might see through her lie. He smoothed her hair, damp from the stream's splash. "Maybe a cupcake will help," she said.

He grinned, leaned over and grabbed a cupcake and held it tantalizingly close to her mouth. When she reached for it, he drew it back.

"Are you going to tease me, a near drowning victim?"

His eyebrow arched. "Put out your tongue."

She did and he swiped the sweet frosting onto it. "Yum," she said, unable to pull her gaze away from his.

"Yes, yum," he repeated, setting the cupcake down and gathering her into his arms. He cradled her there, stroking her hair.

She couldn't break the spell of his eyes. "I must look awful."

"You're beautiful," he countered, running long fingers down her cheek.

She shivered, but not because of the cold water. His touch muddied her mind, making the image of the boy— what was his name?—fade into a fog. Heath's touch also sent a slow sensuous warmth over her skin. She lay against his chest, her heart picking up speed as his fingers slowly worked magic on her body. She closed her eyes, took deep breaths and tried to remember why she'd fallen into the stream. She felt his hand cup her chin, felt his lips brush her temple.

"I love you, Sarah," he said.

Her eyes flew open. Familiar words. Where had she heard them before? Heath's eyes were as clear as rain-water. "You hardly know me," she managed to say, fighting hard to not fall into the consuming desire he had created inside her.

His lips moved down her throat, into the hollow where her pulse throbbed and her breaths grew shallow. She felt languid, unable to pull away. "I know you well enough to know I love you. To know I want you to stay with me." His words quivered against the pulse in her neck.

"Stay with you? Here?"

"Is it such a bad place? Haven't I made you happy?"

"Yes, but—" Her body was on fire for him, yet she realized that pieces of her were still missing. She remembered the stream. When she'd walked into the water . . . Something had happened to her in the water. . . .

"My family can be your family. Stay with me and my history becomes yours."

She felt like she was melting, merging into Heath. "I— I don't know. . . ."

"Tell me you'll stay. Say the words."

Her head lolled back and Heath's mouth searched the hollow of her throat, traveled slowly, ever slowly upward, tasting and licking her skin as he moved toward her lips.

"Kiss me," he said. "Let me taste your breath."

If she let him kiss her, she would be lost. If she fell into him, there would be no climbing out. She could deny him nothing. The trees overhead swayed with a breeze. Blue sky fluttered through layers of lacy leaves. And the face reappeared. The face from the water, Justin's face, ever smiling, his expression ever loving.

With a superhuman effort Sarah gasped and rolled out of Heath's arms and onto the blanket, trembling.

Heath cried, "What happened?"

"I—I can't make promises to you," she said, catching her breath. "Please don't make me."

His eyes went dark, then, as he visibly controlled his anger, faded to a lighter shade of gray. "I didn't mean to force you."

"No, no, it's me." She stood, threw off the blanket, shook her head to clear out the cobwebs and plant Justin's image in her mind. "I'm freezing. Can we go back to the house now? I need to change clothes."

Heath's eyes darkened once more to the color of charcoal. He stared down at his hands. She'd wounded him. "I thought you cared for me," he said.

She couldn't bear to hear the hurt in his voice. "Please, can we talk about this later? I need some time."

"Of course."

She started throwing leftover food into the basket.

"Don't," Heath said. "I'll send someone to clean up."

What mysterious someone would that be? she wondered. Ghost people? She mounted Lethe, glanced skyward. It was growing dark and she could no longer see Justin in the sky above.

Sarah paced in her room like a caged cat, her mind going over the day with Heath. Something was going on that was beyond her ability to understand or control. She felt a powerful attraction to Heath. A visceral, primitive attraction that scared her. He was mysterious, inscrutable, and he made her forget coherent thought when he took her in his arms, or when he touched her with his cool slender hands.

And yet she couldn't forget the face in the water. Her heart had reacted wildly to the face. Her soul had sung out to him, this Justin, this face she recognized but couldn't place. He was locked inside her memory and she had no key, no way in.

The ride back to the stables had been silent, the air between her and Heath strained. At the stable, when she'd dismounted and began to unsaddle Lethe, Heath had said, "Leave it," in a crisp terse voice that sounded sharp.

She left him, hurried to the house and up the stairs to her room, where she lay on the bed and wept. She felt muddled and drained, confused by roiling emotions. She was being torn apart. She hoped Heath wouldn't want to see her again this night.

Once she stopped crying, she rose from the bed and peeled off the still-damp jeans. She found the long night-gown she'd been wearing freshened and neatly folded in a drawer and carried it into the bathroom that adjoined her room. The floor was cold, making her teeth chatter. She glanced at her image in the vanity mirror and was startled by what she saw.

Her face looked gaunt and her eyes sunken, stamped by dark half circles, like bruises that hadn't healed. She leaned closer to the mirror; it was old, and much of the silver coating was off the backside—but how would that explain why she looked so pale and thin? She looked in that same mirror every morning. Why hadn't she noticed before now? She ate her fill at every meal and rode in the sunlight every day. And yet she looked awful . . . as pale as milk. She stepped back from her image, pulled on the gown and padded into the bedroom, trying to erase what she'd seen. What's happening to me?

She went to the windows, heard the wind howling outside and the spit of rain bouncing like marbles hitting the glass. Heath's good to me, she told herself. He'd been kind and generous, sharing his estate, his horses, his woods and meadows, and now he had offered her himself, his name and heritage, his love.

He's shared everything he owns, Sarah told herself.

She should be grateful. She should be crazy for him. Then she was struck by another thought. He'd shared everything and every place on his vast land except one. The only place he'd told her never to go.

The maze.

9

Sarah realized instantly what she must do. She had to explore the maze, but without Heath's knowing. She was certain she'd never get his permission or his approval. She'd have to sneak her way in. It was an underhanded thing to do, but it was the only thing she could think of. There was something about the maze that was different from anyplace else on the estate. Heath had stressed that it was dangerous, and maybe that was true. She needed to explore it for herself, though. Maybe she'd come out of it just fine. "Or," she told herself aloud, "maybe I'll get lost in it forever for the buzzards to find me."

She stood in the dark listening to the wind and pelting rain, begging both to stop before morning. If she was going, it had to be before sunrise. Urgency filled her head and heart. When the rain sounds ceased and only the wind sounds remained, Sarah decided to make her break for the maze.

She put on a couple of sweaters, boots and jeans, grabbed candles and opened her bedroom door quietly. The hall was dimly lit by candle sconces. She hugged the wall to the staircase and crept down the stone steps, watchful for any movement. Perhaps the ghostly "helpers" only worked at night. She didn't want to be seen. She didn't want to have to explain why she was creeping around in the mansion alone when she should be sleeping.

She paused at the front door, changed her mind about using it and instead crept to the morning room, then through the kitchen—where no one ever seemed to be working—and rummaged for a box of matches. She tucked a box into her jeans pocket and, clutching the candles, eased out the door. The wind howled around the corner of the great house and whipped through her clothing as if it were silk, not wool. She shuddered, clenched her teeth so they wouldn't chatter.

There was no moon. The night was pitch black. She was glad for the cover of darkness. And she was glad she'd ridden the property so much with Heath. She knew her way around. Her eyes adjusted and she was surprised at the acuity of her night vision. Sarah moved swiftly, taking a wide turn around the stables. She didn't want the horses catching her scent and sounding an alarm of neighs and snorts. She headed down a slope toward the gardens and was rewarded by the sweet aroma of flowers. Her sense of direction had been right on, and she rewarded herself with "Good going, girl" under her breath.

In spite of the dark, she made out the looming shape of the hedge that formed the maze. She placed her palms on the bushes and inched her way along until she discovered the doorway entrance, only to feel a chain zigzagging across it. She stopped short. Heath had done what she'd advised him to do—barred the opening. "Dumb idea, Sarah," she told herself. Why had he listened to her? Why had she suggested it?

She searched for a gap in the chain big enough to wiggle through, tugging and pushing the metal links as she did. She was able to wiggle the links more freely in the chain's center and soon had worked an opening big enough for her to slip through. Inside the maze, it was even darker, but the wind was gone, held back by the thick snarl of boxwood leaves and branches. Sarah's cold fingers fumbled with a candle and matches, finally getting the wick to ignite and throw feeble light in front of her.

The sides of the maze rose very high, but the path was clean and solid. For a little-used place, it was surprisingly clear of growth and clutter. She had no trouble following the stone path, and she peered ahead anxiously, waiting for the first dead end, the first jog that might trap her if she took it. "What are you looking for?" she asked herself. No answer, because she didn't know.

She came to a junction. Right or left? She closed her eyes, trying to decide. And then she heard voices, whispers, using her name and telling her to "Come." Without hesitation, she turned toward the voices, pushing the candle and its pale light forward. At every turn in the path she paused, closed her eyes and concentrated on the voices. They were leading her. But where?

As the volume of the voices increased, she picked up her pace. She told herself that she had to get to them. She had to make them hear her. She had to discover who they were and why she felt such an urgency to be with them. The voice she now knew to be Justin's kept saying he loved her and that he needed her. Her heart thumped against her chest because although she had only a vague recollection of him, she was sure that he was a part of her past, that she needed him too.

She wove through the paths confidently, no longer fearing dead ends. With the voices at their loudest, she burst around a corner and skidded to a stop. In front of her stood a wall of solid stone. She recalled Heath's telling her that a wall surrounded his estate.

Sarah blinked in disbelief. She'd been certain that she would discover a group of people who knew her, confident that the sight of them would bring back her memory, fill in her blank spaces, tell her who she was and where she'd come from. Instead she faced a wall that stretched so high above her that she knew she couldn't climb over it. She pressed her ear against the hard stone. The voices were muffled and fading. She threw herself against the wall, beat the surface until her fists throbbed painfully. "I'm here!" she yelled. "Listen to me! I'm right here. It's me, Sarah!"

"They can't hear you," a voice said from behind her.

She whirled and stood face to face with Heath de Charon.

He carried a torch that threw crackling fiery light around his head. Heath wore a long black cape with a hood that covered his head. Only his face shone from the depths of the hood—pallid skin and inky black eyes. He asked, "What are you doing here, Sarah? I warned you to stay away from the maze."

Her heart almost jumped out of her chest. She squared her shoulders, lowered her candle with its pitiful smear of light. "I'm trying to get over this wall. There are people on the other side. They keep calling out to me."

"How long have you been hearing their voices?" His question sounded patronizing.

"I'm not crazy. I hear them. I have for . . . for"—she shrugged in frustration because she really had no concept of time anymore—"days," she finished lamely.

"And you never told me about them before now? Didn't you trust me?"

She refused to apologize. "Listen! Can't you hear them?"

Heath leveled his gaze at her. Behind her the voices had grown silent.

She spun, pounded on the stone. "I'm here! It's Sarah!"

"Aren't you happy here with me, Sarah? I've offered

you everything I own. I want you to stay with me forever."

A chill shot up her back. "I'm thankful for everything.
I really am. But . . . but there's something on the other
side of this wall that I need to go to. People who know me
and love me and who want me too." She took a deep
breath. "And people I want to be with more than anything." There. She'd said it. She'd told him what was in
her heart.

He stepped toward her, held out his hand. "Give me
your hand, Sarah."

She knew better. Something murky happened to her
thoughts when he touched her. "No!" she cried, pressing
her back to the wall. "Please don't touch me."

The torch in his hand flared. Sarah's stomach twisted
in a knot. She didn't know what he was going to do. He
was stronger and could overpower her, drag her away
from the wall, force her to return to his home, force her
to become his alone. Except that he didn't. He simply
stared, as if rooted to the ground. "I want you, Sarah.
Come with me."

And then she realized something. He couldn't make
her go with him. That was the whole point of their meals
together, the rides on fleet horses, the evenings in front
of the fireplace, the picnic in the woods. He couldn't
make her stay. He had to persuade her to stay. He had to
make her believe that staying was what she wanted.

The insight emboldened her. She said, "You need me to tell you I want you too, don't you?"

Heath stood silent, his eyes dark orbs and his face an expressionless mask.

She pressed harder into the wall and could have sworn the stones were growing softer. Impossible. "For some reason I have to agree to stay with you, don't I? Why, Heath? Why are you trying so hard to make me agree that you're what I want?"

His expression turned thunderous, and wind whipped up, seeping through the hedge and blowing his cape. The torchlight danced but didn't extinguish. "Don't you know who I am?"

"*H-e-a-t-h.*" She spelled his name out loud, substituting one letter for another—the *H* for a *D*. "Death," she whispered, her knees going weak. "You're Death and you want me to stay here. But for some reason I still have a choice."

He said nothing. She knew she was correct. She could leave.

She pressed her hands flat against the wall and felt the stones getting warmer and softer. The wall was turning pliable at her back.

The wind stopped. Silence reigned. Heath lowered his hood and she saw him in the light of the flame in all his cold terrible beauty. The black curls of hair. The smooth skin and sharp planes of his face and chiseled jaw, his full sensual lips. "I always win, Sarah," he said quietly. "You can leave now, but I'll come for you again."

"Not until I'm a very old woman," she said defiantly, holding her chin high.

Behind her the wall had become as soft as feathers. Heath reached for her. She pushed backward and went into free fall through the wall and into total blackness.

10

Sarah woke in a room, in a bed with white sheets and a machine beside it. She blinked, trying to bring the room into focus. She heard a chair scrape nearby and then Justin's face appeared above her.

"Oh my God! You're awake! Oh, baby. You're awake."

She tried to speak but couldn't.

"Don't," he shouted. "You have a tube down your throat. A doctor has to take it out." He picked up a remote and pressed a button over and over. "I'll get a nurse. Oh, Sarah . . . . oh my gosh, you're awake. Your mom and dad just went down to the cafeteria. I—I'll go get them." He got as far as the door, turned and ran back to her bed. He picked up her hand, kissed it. "No. I'm not going anywhere. Where's that nurse?"

Sarah gathered her strength and squeezed his hand. She watched tears form in his eyes. She wanted to say, "It's okay. I'm okay," but of course, she couldn't speak.

Justin bent, kissed her cheek and allowed himself to cry against her hair.

It took several hours before Sarah was cognizant enough to hear what had happened to her. The story fell on her in bits and pieces, first from her exuberant parents, then from Justin and then doctors. One doctor pulled the tube from her throat. It hurt like crazy, but she could breathe on her own, and in a voice made raspy by the extraction of the tube past her vocal cords, she told her family and Justin she loved them.

Her mother couldn't stop sobbing happy tears and her dad couldn't stop smiling. But no matter who was in the room, Sarah's eyes kept connecting with Justin's.

She heard how she'd gotten sick—she vaguely remembered having a sore throat and terrible headache, a fever so high that she shivered uncontrollably, a stiff neck—and how she'd fallen unconscious on the family sofa. "I was fixing your lunch." Her mom recounted Sarah's ordeal. "When I found you, when I couldn't wake you up, I called an ambulance."

She'd been rushed to the hospital, diagnosed with encephalitis, a swelling of her brain brought on by an infection. "You slipped into a coma," her dad said.

"How long?" Sarah rasped.

"Ten days," her mother answered.

Incredulous, Sarah glanced at the doctor. "You were one sick girl," he said. "We started you on IV antibiotics, intubated you, fed you via a feeding tube. Comas can be difficult, but I believed you'd come out of it. You're young and generally healthy."

"I heard your voices," she said, her own voice little more than a whisper.

Her parents and Justin shared a knowing look. Justin said, "Researchers say that people in comas can often hear. They say that people who come out of comas tell them that they sometimes heard and remembered what people in the room said. So we devised a plan to talk to you and read to you round the clock."

Sarah's dad clapped Justin on the shoulder. "His idea. I'm glad we did it."

"You read me stories," Sarah said to her dad. "I remember that much."

Her dad looked sheepish. "Picture books, fairy tales from when you were a little girl. Your favorites."

"I just jabbered," her mom confessed. "I told every family story I ever knew."

Sarah blinked back tears. "I heard you talking. I tried to tell you but you couldn't hear me."

Justin jammed his hands into his jeans pockets. His face reddened and he dropped his gaze. "I—um—just talked."

"You said you loved me."

His redness deepened and he cut his eyes self-consciously toward her parents. "I did. I do."

"You brought me back."

Justin broke into a face-splitting smile. Sarah's mother hugged him and Sarah closed her eyes in gratitude.

"Where were you? When you were in the coma, I mean," Justin asked. "I could see your body on the bed. You twitched. You moaned. But you didn't wake up. So where was your mind? Was it like a dream?"

Sarah was home again, still weak, but home with her family. "I don't know," she said. "It's all just a big blank spot in my head."

She and Justin sat on her living room sofa together. Her books and computer and notepads were strewn over the top of the coffee table. Her mother had told her, "I left everything as you'd left it. I couldn't bear to move anything. I'd look at it, think about you touching it, and I'd start to cry. I just walked away."

Sarah picked up a book. *Wuthering Heights,* by Emily Brontë. She thumbed the pages. The name Heathcliff jumped out at her. Something familiar and yet not quite right. "I was working on an essay for English Lit," Sarah said.

"I think it's overdue," Justin said. His brown eyes danced with mischief. "Although I think you can get an

extension. I mean, a coma . . . that's a pretty good excuse."

She swatted his arm. "Very funny."

"Here," Justin said, thrusting the milk shake that he'd
brought at her. "Your doc doesn't want you scrimping on
calories."

Sarah had lost weight during her ordeal. Her jeans and
tees hung on her. She took the shake and sipped it.
"Thanks for bringing this over."

"Any excuse to see you."

Her brow puckered. "Do you know the word *Charon*?"

"Nope. Why?"

"I'm not sure. It's just stuck in my head."

"I'll do a Web search." Justin picked up her laptop,
turned it on and, once the machine had booted up, tapped
the word into a search engine. "According to the online
dictionary it comes from Greek mythology. Charon was
the ferryman who took the souls of the dead into Hades."

Sarah made a face. "Gross. How about *Lethe*? That
word's nagging me too."

Justin tapped the keys. "It's also Greek. Means 'forget-
fulness.' A river in Hades. The souls who drank the water
forgot everything." He looked up. "Geez, creepy words."

Sarah made a face. The definitions left her feeling
creeped out, and she had no idea why the words had
popped into her head. "Did Dad read any mythology
to me?"

"Naw . . . just fairy tales. 'Cinderella,' 'Sleeping

Beauty'—they're all the same. The girl ends up with Prince Charming. Boring."

"Girls love princess stories. We all want to meet our Prince Charming."

"How about me? Do I make the cut?" He waggled his eyebrows.

He looked so adorable, she laughed. "You can't be Prince Charming. You have no kingdom, no castle, no beautiful horse."

He hung his head. "So I'm a loser."

She kissed him. "Not totally."

Justin closed the computer. "Walk me to your door."

"Do you have to leave?"

"I promised your mom I wouldn't stay long. You're still recuperating, you know."

They walked to the front door hand in hand. Justin opened it and she stepped outside with him. He held her, kissed her deeply. "I'm so glad you're back."

"Me too." His arms felt cozy and his breath tasted like mint.

He headed to the driveway, opened his car door. "My faithful horse," he said over his shoulder.

She laughed. "Good night, Prince Charming." She stood and watched the taillights of his car disappear down the street.

Sarah took deep breaths, looked upward. The night sky was studded with stars. Thin wispy clouds skittered across the moon, which was huge, perfectly divided in half, one side aglow with luminous white light, the other half pitch black. It was either coming or going toward fullness. She didn't know which.

All at once an apparition appeared that stole her breath.

She saw the ghostly features of a male face, his skin icy pale and his deep-set eyes clear as glass, the color of rain.

Sarah jumped backward, her heart thudding uncontrollably. A chill sent shivers up her body and her blood turned cold. As quickly as the face had appeared, it dissolved. Only a trick of the night sky, she told herself. Wasn't it? She turned, opened the door of her house and hurried into the warmth and light. I'll see my Prince Charming tomorrow, she thought, and shut the door tight.

When the Clock Chimes

For of all sad words of tongue or pen, the saddest are these: "It might have been!"

—John Greenleaf Whittier (1807–1892)

1

WANTED: Literate teen for summer work. Organized and efficient. Tasks include cataloging artifacts for college professor. Good hourly wage. Applicant must apply in person. 13 Sand stone Mountain.

Drake Iverson looked at the ad for the first job he'd been interested in pursuing in his two-week-long daily search. Not a lot out there for sixteen-year-olds, especially sixteen-year-olds like him.

He heard his mother clatter down the stairs of their townhome, and he glanced up at the clock on the kitchen wall.

She burst into the kitchen, throwing him a harried look. "I know I'm running late. The alarm didn't go off—forgot to change the batteries, and I knew they were low."

She ran to the pot of coffee that Drake had already brewed and filled her travel mug. "Got to go."

"Whoa," Drake said. He was sitting at the kitchen counter that jutted into the family room and served as their informal table. "There's always time for breakfast." That was what she always said to him when he was running late on school days.

"Ha-ha," she said.

Drake shoved a protein bar toward her. "Eat this in the car, Mom. You'd never let me run off without breakfast."

She juggled her coffee mug and briefcase, snatched up the food bar, got to the doorway and paused. "You going to be all right all day alone?"

"Haven't I always been?"

"You should go out and explore."

They'd been in Sanderson, North Carolina, for three weeks. His mother had taken a new and better job there in May and moved them to the town nestled in the Smokies as soon as Drake had finished his sophomore year. Drake knew she felt guilty about moving him away from Ohio and his school and his friends. It wasn't a big deal to Drake. He'd only had a few friends anyway, and he could attend school anyplace. No love lost between him and Ohio. His consolation prize for the move had been his own car. It wasn't hot or sporty, but it did give him mobility.

"I'm going to take a look at this job in today's paper. You know where Sandstone Mountain is?"

"Not a clue."

"I'll Google it."

"Be careful."

He rolled his shoulders. "Aren't I always?"

She came back to the table and kissed his cheek. "I love you."

"I'll start dinner," he said, shrugging her off. "Spaghetti okay?"

"Hamburger's already thawed. You call me anytime."

She left and Drake slid off the stool and lurched awkwardly toward the desk and computer set up in the family room. He'd been born with cerebral palsy, a birth defect that marked him for life. His left leg was short, and underdeveloped muscles caused a permanent rocking limp. He was spastic, a crip, a gimp, a weirdo. He'd heard all of these terms for himself over the years from the perfectly formed, the physically elite. Many kids with CP were in worse shape; only one of Drake's legs was affected. He had no learning problems, no uncontrollable tremors, no tendency to drool. Still he'd been branded a "retard" by those with fleshly symmetry.

Drake turned on the computer and waited for it to boot up. In elementary school his mother had protected him as if he were her wounded wolf cub, even going so far as instituting a schoolwide CP Day to "spread understanding" when he'd been in the second grade. He remembered the embarrassment of being singled out, of hearing kids whisper about him in the halls and cafeteria.

She'd meant well, but CP Day had been a nightmare for him. Once he'd hit middle and high school, the last thing he'd wanted was his mother hovering over him and running interference on his behalf. So he took the teasing and jabs from peers stoically.

The computer screen glowed and Drake called up the Internet, then a map search of Sandstone Mountain. The mountain was sparsely populated, a mecca for wealthy summer residents, and houses were far apart, surrounded by woods. He found homes numbered twelve and fourteen, a good ten miles apart from one another. There was no number thirteen. He grumbled, wondered if the newspaper had given the wrong address, and printed a map. He'd go to both addresses and ask for the professor who'd placed the ad. It was probably a sit-down job, one a cripple like him could handle. He didn't want to spend the summer trapped at home, but he wasn't ready to try for an out-in-the-public grunt job either. He wanted *this* job.

The road up Sandstone was paved—mostly. Drake drove carefully. He'd grown up in a flat part of Ohio, so he wasn't used to the mountain curves. The higher he got, the rougher the road became. It went from paved to pea-rock to rutted dirt. He finally saw a sign that directed him to number thirteen and a hidden driveway. The Internet mapmakers had missed a house. At the foot of the hidden driveway, overgrown shrubs and vines halted his car.

A handwritten sign on a fence gate read: NO AUTOS BE-YOND THIS POINT. NO TRESPASSING.

"Great. Just great," Drake grumbled. He'd have to go the rest of the way on foot. Not easy, but he'd manage. He wedged his car into a weed-infested opening beside the dirt road and started up the path, hoping it wouldn't be too difficult for him navigate. The air this high up was cooler than in the city, and felt good to him. He climbed, rounded a curve, edged a clump of trees and stopped short, breathing hard. His bad leg trembled with exertion. The view was amazing but had remained completely hidden until he'd come out of the bend in the path.

A house built of gray river stone, with a long porch and a turret that jutted into the blue sky, stood on a stretch of manicured lawn bordered by a white picket fence. Blooming hydrangeas, their flowery heads drooping in the sun, surrounded the porch. The house was impressive—Drake had studied architecture, hoping to become an architect one day.

He stood staring because the house and grounds looked picture-perfect, the colors so saturated and pure that the scene resembled a photograph. Thirteen Sandstone Mountain was a vision from another era.

He made his way to a gate beneath a trellis heavy with wisteria vines and limped up a flagstone walkway to the porch, where he grabbed the handrail, pulled himself up the steps and rang the front bell.

The door was opened by a portly man with a brown

beard and bushy eyebrows. He smelled of pipe tobacco. "Yes?"

"Um—I'm here about your ad," Drake stammered. "The cataloging job."

The man eyed him. "You had no trouble finding my house?"

"Drove right here," Drake said. No need to mention that the Web maps had no record of the address. Plus, if anyone else applied, they might not be so lucky about finding the place.

The man studied Drake keenly, then held out his hand. "I'm Avery Dennison, professor of archaeology at Harvard."

"Drake Iverson."

"Come in."

Drake stepped into the house. Its design and dark wood floor, doorframes and moldings were reminiscent of another century. "Wow," he said, then caught himself and added, "Nice place. I—I like architecture."

"Our summer place," the professor said. "We like to get out of Cambridge and the heat. I like the mountains."

Drake nodded. He hated adult small talk, but he wanted to make a good impression. "About the job," he said.

"Yes, of course. How old are you, Mr. Iverson?"

"Almost seventeen. And I'm literate."

The professor chuckled. "I only wanted serious applicants." Behind the professor, in the hallway, stood an ancient grandfather clock that chimed nine o'clock. Drake assumed it was wrong. He'd left his house at nine, and the drive had taken him forty minutes.

Just then, a door in the back of the house opened and Drake saw someone approaching down the long shotgun-style hallway. A girl with an armload of flowers came into the foyer. The professor turned and stepped aside. "My daughter, Regina," Professor Dennison said.

All the air left Drake's lungs. The girl was about his age, with white blond hair that fell past her shoulders, big blue eyes and the face of an angel.

She smiled warmly at Drake. "Hello."

"Hi," he managed to say.

Dennison beamed his daughter a glorious smile. "Good news, Gina. I've just hired Mr. Iverson for the summer."

2

Drake blinked. He had hardly gone through a real interview and yet just like that he'd been hired. It wasn't what he'd expected, but he was glad he'd gotten the job. "Um—thanks. What do you need me to do?"

"Follow me."

"You're not going to stick Drake in our nasty old basement, are you, Daddy?" Gina asked.

"It's not so terrible," Dennison said. "Besides, it's where the boxes of my artifacts are stored."

"I don't mind," Drake said, feeling his face heat up. Gina was so pretty; he wished she'd leave so that she wouldn't have to see him follow with his limping, lurching gait.

He'd never forget the day in seventh grade when Sheila Morgan had sidled up to him in the cafeteria and said, "Hey, you're cute. Are you new?"

Several schools had been funneled into the newly built

middle and high school at that time. Drake had looked up from his textbook and half-eaten sandwich into her dark brown eyes. He'd never met her, but everybody knew Sheila, the most popular girl in the school. Drake had stammered and Sheila had glanced around at her clique of friends and said, "I may let you walk me to my next class." The bevy of girls snickered and poked each other.

And Drake momentarily forgot himself, stood up and stepped toward her. His chair teetered backward and he stumbled forward, catching himself on the table as his leg buckled. The look of disdain on Sheila's face was one he'd never forgotten. She'd flipped her hair off her shoulder and said, "Maybe tomorrow," and swished away, her friends buzzing around her like worker bees around the queen. Now, years later, he didn't want to see that look cross Gina's face.

"Come on," Dennison said.

Gina stepped up next to Drake. He moved slowly, trying to control his rocking gait and conceal his handicap as much as possible.

"Daddy is a dear," Gina whispered. "But he's a slave driver." She smiled and Drake's heart melted. She hardly seemed to notice the way he walked.

The basement was down a flight of stone stairs that left Drake straining and his legs wobbly. He worried that the stairs might disqualify him from the job—and from Gina's attention.

The basement was lit by lamps—Tiffany lamps, he was certain of that—and a bare overhead bulb. Two tall stacks of brown boxes lined a back wall. A fire crackled in a small woodstove in a corner, mingling the smell of smoke with damp and must. Gina wrinkled her nose. "Daddy—"

"This is fine, sir," Drake said quickly. "All I need is direction."

"Yes, well, there's a lot to do before we return to Harvard after Labor Day."

Gina leaned toward Drake. "I'll bring fresh flowers for you every day." She dropped the bundle she carried next to a cut-glass vase on an old table.

"That's nice of you. But I'll be all right down here."

The professor walked to the stack of boxes and opened one, withdrawing an Indian arrowhead with a tag attached. "These are from an old archaeological dig in the Northeast. I need you to accurately record each artifact by date and tribe. These boxes represent the culture of tribes all the way to the Midwest, and the boxes are in a jumble, without order, so I need everything recorded legibly in chronological order. Most of the boxes have a date span marked on the outside, but every piece must be verified and matched to this master sheet." He held up a sheaf of faded paper. "I'm writing a textbook, so accuracy matters."

Tedious work, Drake thought, but not difficult. "All

right." He glanced around the basement. "Where's your computer?"

"Our what?" Gina asked.

"Everything must be recorded by hand in this book." Dennison picked up a thick ledger with leather covers.

"You're serious?" Drake said before he could stop himself. "I can bring a laptop from home—"

Dennison shook his head. "Sorry. There's no way to get such things to work up here. This house isn't wired for much more than basic electricity."

"I just need to plug it in and turn it on. I'll record everything, save it to a file."

"No," Dennison said firmly. "I want it done by hand."

Without a computer, the job took on a new complexity. "When can I start?" Drake hoped he sounded eager and enthusiastic, not the way he really felt about the job.

"Start tomorrow," Dennison said. "Be here by nine. Leave at four."

"I won't be late."

Drake slid his cell phone from his pocket, checking the time. The screen was dark, which he thought odd because it had been fully charged when he'd left home. He understood that there might not be cell service up here, but he didn't understand why the timekeeping function had stopped working. He shook the phone, embarrassed.

"There is a grandfather clock upstairs. It will let you know when it's four o'clock every day without fail."

Drake couldn't imagine not depending on his cell, but he shrugged and said, "I'll listen for it."

Back upstairs, Drake again looked at the clock. It appeared too old and decrepit to keep time, but the hands were pointing to eleven o'clock. He did some quick math—if he'd left home around eight-fifteen, arrived at nine according to the old clock and it now read eleven, the clock really was screwy. He couldn't believe he'd been here two hours already. On cue, the clock chimed, the sound clear and melodious as a bell. He shook the professor's hand.

Gina opened the front door for him. "See you tomorrow."

Her smile was radiant, and Drake felt a tug on his heart. He returned to his car telling himself to stop imagining the impossible. Girls like Gina were dream fodder. He'd known since preschool that bias against the handicapped was never stronger than among his own kind.

"I'm telling you, Mom, that house has to be seventy-five or eighty years old." Drake and his mother sat at the kitchen counter eating spaghetti and meat sauce. He'd filled her in on his new job.

"There are a lot of old houses in this area."

"Maybe so, but number thirteen didn't look that old. I'm serious. The furniture looked new, the floors all shiny."

"It's probably a replica. New builds can look old if the homeowner's willing to spend the money," his mother said. "Although I don't care too much for your sitting in a damp basement all day. Promise you'll take your lunch and eat outside in the sunshine."

Drake dropped his head in exasperation. "Mom, I've got a job to do—it's not supposed to be a day at the beach. I want to keep this job."

"And I'm glad for you, but can it hurt to take some time for lunch outside?"

Drake recognized her protective instincts, so he changed the subject. "Listen, communication isn't the best up there." Who was he kidding? It was nonexistent. "No cell service, no wireless. They may not even have a phone. This guy likes his privacy."

She frowned. "I don't like knowing we can't get hold of each other."

"I'll send up smoke signals if you want."

She eyed him humorlessly. "What's this man paying you to sit in his basement and wade through old musty boxes?"

Drake felt heat crawl up his neck. He'd never asked. How could he confess that Gina had distracted him to the point that he'd have taken the job for free? No need to mention Gina to his mother at this time. "Enough," he said. "It isn't rocket science."

"Is this how you really want to spend your summer? In a basement by yourself pawing through artifacts instead of having fun, maybe meeting kids you'll be going to school with?"

People who were perfectly formed couldn't identify with people like him. Drake had CP. He was broken. Damaged. Invisible to most of the able-bodied. "Yes," Drake said firmly. "This is exactly what I want to do."

3

The next morning, Drake parked his car in the brush and retraced his steps from the day before to the great house. The house looked razor sharp against the brilliant blue sky. Gina waited at the gate beneath the trellis, the purple wisteria swaying in the early summer breeze above her head. She waved and he grinned and waved back.

"Hi," she said, swinging the gate open for him. "We have a surprise for you."

She was his surprise. "I like surprises."

She fell into step next to him. He felt awkward at first, but once more, she didn't seem to care how crazily he walked. Inside the house, she called, "Daddy, Drake's here." She led Drake into the first room off the hallway. "This used to be the dining room, but with only me and Daddy living here, it was expendable. We turned it into a library, and now, your workroom."

The room glowed sunny and bright from a large bow window. Floor-to-ceiling bookcases stretched along one wall, and a long oak table had been set up in the middle of the room. Boxes were stacked like steps on a third wall.

"Are those the boxes from the basement?" Drake asked.

Gina nodded. "I told Daddy it was wrong to make you work down there like a mole, so we moved the boxes."

He wondered if his handicap had spurred them to make the change. Embarrassing. An old man and a girl catering to his problem. What next? A ramp up the porch? "Did you and the professor carry them up?"

"No, silly," she said. "We have a dumbwaiter in the hall-way. We loaded the boxes and brought them up here."

A dumbwaiter—a device once used in old houses to move goods and food between floors before elevators. It made sense, but he still felt inadequate. "I like this room better."

"Me too."

Dennison bustled into the room. "Good morning."

"I like the move upstairs," Drake said. "Thanks."

Dennison waved him off. "Let's get you started."

Drake crossed to the table just as the clock in the hall chimed. He counted the gongs silently while listening to the professor's instructions. He heard eight gongs. Impossible. He'd left his house at eight o'clock to drive here and yet now the clock was chiming eight. Yesterday it had been right on the money about hitting eleven, but now it was off by over an hour. It was the weirdest clock he'd ever been around.

"When you leave, no need to hunt for me—I'm often preoccupied in the afternoons." He turned away. "Until tomorrow, then. Same time."

Drake watched them both leave the room. He sighed and limped over to the pile of boxes, heaved one onto the table and set to work.

By noon, Drake had hardly made headway on the first box. Reading the old, brittle and faded labels attached to each artifact was difficult, and recording each on paper by hand was intense slow work. He didn't want to make a mistake, so he checked and double-checked his spellings and descriptions before laying each piece aside. He missed his computer, where it was easy to correct errors.

He worked in silence, hearing the chime of the clock every hour. He decided that not having Gina around him while he worked was probably a good thing; her presence would have distracted him. He felt a powerful attraction to her. Usually he became invisible once girls saw his deformity—a pathetic truth he'd learned to face. Yet when he looked into Gina's eyes, he felt whole. Stupid, he told himself. There were no jocks around to impress her. No other guys vying for her attention. Hadn't she told him she and her father lived alone in the house?

When Drake's stomach growled, he stretched, laid down his pencil and picked up his bag lunch. He decided

to go outside because he wanted to check out the place—
not because his mother had asked him to. He went around
to the backyard and found a wooden bench in the middle
of a path surrounded by colorful gardens. Roses scented
the air and bees hummed around flower heads. Sunshine
warmed his back.

"How do you like my gardens?"

He looked up to see Gina on the path, her hands full
of gardening tools. The sun's rays bounced off her dazzling white blond hair like dancing fireflies and made his
heart skip.

"Beautiful," he said, telling her two things at once.

She laughed and settled beside him on the bench.
"Want some lemonade? I made it this morning. I can run
up to the kitchen for it."

"I'm good," he said, not wanting her to leave, not even
for a drink of something cool.

She dropped her tools and pulled off her gloves,
smoothed her skirt.

"Are you in charge of these gardens?"

"I keep them up. I love flowers, don't you?"

"Sure," he said, watching her hands flutter like bird
wings as she talked.

"How's the work going?"

"Slow. Be better if I had a computer. Don't you miss
having one up here?"

She smiled politely but looked as if the words didn't
register for her.

"You do have a computer back home, don't you?"

"Father's not keen on some things." She glanced away, turned back and changed the conversation with, "Tell me about yourself."

"Not much to tell. I moved here at the end of May. Before that, we were in Ohio."

"What about your family?"

"I live with my mother." He didn't want to confess that he'd never known a father because his mother had never married. She'd just gone her own way, having her baby and raising him by herself. He'd stopped asking questions about his father years before. "How about you? Where's your mom?"

"She died giving birth to me."

Gina sounded sad, making him wish he hadn't asked. "Sorry."

She shrugged, smiled. "Father's done everything in the world to make me happy."

Drake got it. He was feeling as if he'd do anything to make her happy too. "I should get back to work," he said, wadding up his paper bag.

"And I have piano to practice," she said.

"I can't play anything except my iPod," he said.

She again gave him a polite disconnected look.

"You don't have an iPod," he said, as if filling in the blank. "A TV?"

She shook her head and looked down at her hands, now stilled. "Just a piano."

He went back inside the house wondering how anyone lived without computers, iPods or TVs. Strange, he thought. But he guessed it was what people got used to that defined their lives. He was glad he didn't have to live without such things.

Drake spent the afternoon cataloging and listening to Gina's piano music. The notes came down the stairs like strangers because the music she played wasn't familiar to Drake at all. Classical, he guessed. Some of the music was fast and almost discordant. Some pieces sounded magnificent and bold, others soft and beguiling. He vowed to search iTunes that evening and become better acquainted with her musical tastes. No place for rock or rap or today's latest bands in Gina's world.

She was still playing when the clock in the hall struck four. Drake looked at the short stack of artifacts he'd recorded and wasn't impressed. He had to work faster. He lingered for a few minutes, hoping Gina would descend the stairs and tell him goodbye. She didn't. He sighed, gathered his sweatshirt and went into the hall. He started toward the door but turned back and hobbled over to the great clock.

The clock was much bigger than it had seemed yesterday, and very old, its wood dry and pockmarked. The face was marked with strange symbols and the hands were made of wood, not metal. Below the face was a boxy case fronted with wavy old glass, and inside was a copper pendulum that slid from side to side ever so slowly. Drake wondered if the clock needed winding. The *tick-tock* sound was mesmerizing, hypnotic. It seemed to him that time was leaking out of it.

He leaned closer, trying to decipher the symbols. He reached into his pocket and drew out his cell, flipped on the camera feature only to see that it wasn't working either. He shook his head in disgust. It had been working just fine before he got to work.

"What are you doing?" Dennison's voice thundered from behind him.

Drake's bad leg almost buckled as he spun. "Nothing," he said. "I—I mean, just looking at your clock."

Dennison's eyes were narrowed and his face looked angry. "Well, get away from it!"

Drake inched around the professor. "Sorry . . . it's unique—"

"Don't go near it, you hear? It's ancient and most delicate. And never touch it."

"Y-yes, sir." Drake turned the front-door knob, stupefied by the depth of the man's anger. He shut the door quickly while Dennison glared at him. His leg hurt like crazy, but he shuffled down the porch steps and out the gate as fast as he could, Gina's music cascading wildly from the upstairs windows, chasing him.

4

Drake returned the next morning, fearful that Dennison would throw him out again, but the house was quiet and his workroom was just as he'd left it. Drake hurried inside and set to work just as the offending clock, the reason for Dennison's explosion, struck eight. "Wrong," Drake muttered under his breath. He'd left home at eight.

For the next few days he worked silently, knocking off at four when the clock chimed. He didn't see the professor, but he did see Gina in the halls. She was like a bright light floating between rooms. When he caught her eye, she smiled shyly but then slipped away. He ate in the garden every day for a week but didn't encounter her again.

By the end of the second week, he hated the work. Without a computer it was painfully slow. The stack of various artifacts of arrowheads, clay pipes, beaded doeskin slippers and hunks of ancient feathers from long-dead

Native American tribes of the Northeast and Midwest wasn't dwindling. How many of these relics did the old man have squirreled away? An arrowhead stabbed his finger and he swore.

"Mind if I visit for a while?" Gina asked from the doorway.

Caught off guard, hoping she hadn't heard his outburst, Drake fumbled the brittle arrowhead.

"I didn't mean to startle you," she said.

"Sure, come in. I love"—he stopped, rephrased—"enjoy your company." He hoped he hadn't sounded too enthusiastic, like the kind of dog that jumps up and down when it gets the least bit of attention.

She smiled brightly. "I enjoy your company too."

His black mood lifted instantly. She was holding a small basket in her hands. "Work project?" he asked, pointing at the basket.

"My embroidery basket. Want to see what I'm doing?"

Of course he did. She pulled a chair over to a large bay window and Drake eased next to her. She lifted a small hoop and a mound of colorful thread from the basket. "I'm embroidering a lady's hanky. Here in this corner, I'm creating a nosegay of purple lilacs. Do you know the Victorian language of flowers?"

He had no clue. He didn't even know what a nosegay was, but he saw that the linen cloth was stretched across the hoop and a cluster of flowers in subtle shades of purple and lavender was taking shape with thread. "Flower language isn't in my dictionary, but the lilacs you're sewing look pretty cool."

Gina smiled shyly. "Every flower, every color has a special meaning. It's how men and women communicated their feelings in Victorian times."

"Like texting? You know, making a few letters or numbers tell somebody something you want to say?"

Gina laughed. "I don't speak texting. Embroidery passes the time for me, and I create something lovely. I never think of it as work."

Living without a TV, computer or iPod, she had to do something in her spare time, Drake supposed.

She began her sewing, and Drake returned to his cataloging tasks, but every few minutes, he'd steal a look at her in the straight-backed chair. Her hair was like spun silver, so white blond that it sparkled. Her face was a study in concentration. Her presence wasn't one bit distracting, as he'd thought it would be.

He said, "I liked the music you were playing yesterday."

"Really?" Her eyes lit up.

"So are you going after a music career?"

Gina laughed. "Goodness no. I'm not good enough."

"I think you are."

"You're kind." She nodded gratefully in his direction.

"So what do you want to do? You know, when you finish school."

"I would love to be a dancer, a ballerina."

"You dance too?" His mother watched some show featuring dancers, and they made it look so easy and fluid. For normal people, dancing might be easy. It was something he could never do.

"I have a studio on the third floor, in the attic," she said, pointing up. "Father built it for me, one giant room with a mirrored wall and a practice barre. It's very nice."

"Will you be a dancer, then?"

"Not likely. I'll probably be a schoolteacher. Like Father, except I'll teach young children. How about you?" she asked. "What are your dreams?"

To have a girl in my life like you, he thought. "Architect," he said.

"Like Frank Lloyd Wright?"

"That is a dream." He grinned.

"I have an idea," Gina said as the clock in the hall chimed noon. "It looks cloudy outside. We'll have a picnic in my dance studio."

His smile froze. Lunch with her would be awesome, but climbing to the attic level would be difficult for him. He didn't want her to see him struggle.

She jammed her needlework into her basket and stood. "I'll get some sandwiches and fruit together. You can go up and wait for me. Tip-top room." She hurried away.

He silently blessed her. She had given him time to

climb the stairs at his own awkward pace. He went into the hall, past the old clock, its hands pointing to high noon, and started up the three flights of stairs.

The attic was huge, with wide-plank oak flooring, a floor-to-ceiling mirror along one wall, windows along another and a small sofa and table tucked in a corner of the room—where Gina could rest, he figured. The table was really a boxy piece of furniture with a lid and a small brass plate that read VICTOR THE TALKING MACHINE. He lifted the lid, saw that it held a turntable and a shiny black disc. A record? He'd seen DJs on MTV playing vinyl in hip-hop contests, but this disc didn't look quite like those records. There was a windup arm on the machine, so he turned it, set the small metal arm on the record and heard music. The sound was awful, tinny and quivery. Primitive. Why was her father so old-fashioned? Geez, why didn't he give Gina a decent machine for her music?

Drake was still fiddling with the machine when Gina popped into the room carrying a tray. "Lunch!" She glided across the floor and placed the tray on the floor in front of the sofa.

"Looks great," he said, eying the thick meat sandwiches. His stomach growled and they laughed in unison.

He sat beside her, picked up a sandwich and nodded toward the machine. "Where did you get that antique?"

"Daddy borrowed it from a friend. For me. So I can have music when I dance."

The music warbled as the windup slowed. "They make better machines, you know."

"No electricity up here," she said. "See? Candles."

Sure enough, at the base of the walls along the floor were rows of candles, most partly burned. Antiques could be valuable, and Gina didn't seem to care if the music machine was ancient. Dennison liked old things, so who was Drake to bad-mouth Dennison's old stuff?

"Food's good," he said, getting off the music topic. She smiled, making his heart trip into double time. How could she do that with just a smile?

Her gaze drifted to the windows and her smile faded. "A storm's coming," she said, putting down her food and standing. "I hate storms."

He followed her gaze, saw black clouds filling the sky. He boosted himself up. "It's just rain."

She shook her head and looked nervous. "Thunder and lightning scare me. Always."

He saw that she was serious. Just then loud thunder broke the silence. She clapped her hands over her ears and ducked against his chest. Instinctively his arm went around her. "It can't hurt you in here." Her body felt warm and soft.

Another roll of thunder made her cower, and he hugged her more tightly. He was thanking the heavens for the storm, for allowing him to hold her, when Dennison's voice roared, "Gina! Where are you?"

She broke away and rushed to the door. "In the studio. Drake's with me."

Drake closed his eyes, certain that the professor would fire him for sure. He was way out of his work zone, alone with Gina, and all without her dad's knowledge. He was dead meat.

Gina grabbed his hand. "Come downstairs." Her eyes were wide with fright.

He had no choice, so he hobbled along behind her, holding the banister and moving as quickly as his leg would allow him. Dennison took Gina into his arms at the bottom of the stairs. The clock chimed five. Drake glared at it. No way they could have been upstairs for five hours!

Dennison looked at him. "You'd better leave," he said.

Drake figured he was being fired. "I—I didn't mean to take so long—"

Dennison waved him off. "Just go while you can. The road will be dangerous."

Drake nodded, weak with relief. He wasn't being fired. "I—I'll see you tomorrow."

Once outside, he turned to look at the house through the curtain of water. An undulating wave seemed to make the grand house quiver from top to bottom, as if the stones were shifting and the image was moving. Impossible. He blinked hard, wiped the rain from his face, certain his eyes were playing tricks on him. In seconds the illusion ceased and the image held firm. Soaked to the skin, Drake hurried to his car, where he sat dripping on the upholstery and wondering what in the world he'd just seen.

5

"Thank heaven you're home," Drake's mom said when he came in the door. "I was worried about you driving in the storm."

He came into the kitchen only to see her sitting at the counter with a woman he'd never met. The other woman was as round as a muffin.

"This is Lois. We work together."

Drake nodded and Lois began to explain. "Power went out at the office around noon, and after an hour in the dark with computers down, the boss told us to go home. When I tried to start my car, the battery was dead, so Connie brought me home with her." Lois grinned gratefully at Drake's mother. "My hubby will come get me when the rain lets up."

"Want some coffee?" his mother asked. "Fresh pot."

"Sure." He limped to the counter, certain that Lois was watching him, maybe feeling pity for him. As he poured his coffee, he caught sight of the time on the coffee machine. Three-thirty. How could that be? He'd left the Dennison's place after five. The clock at the old house was nutso. Right sometimes, wrong sometimes.

Lois said, "Connie tells me you're working for a Harvard professor who lives up on Sandstone."

"That's right."

"I keep trying to visualize the house, but I can't. Harold and I used to drive all around up there looking at the fine homes. The houses are like palaces, just gorgeous. I can't quite get a bead on the place where you're working."

"It has a Craftsman-Gothic vibe, made mostly of river stone and wood. There's a turret on one side. And a big porch. And lots of flower gardens."

Lois puckered her brow. "Can't picture it."

"It's hard to find. I have to park below the house and climb up a road and around a bend. I almost gave up the first time I hunted for it."

"Did you have a good day?" his mother asked.

"Yeah, fine. Not a lot of excitement cataloging Native American artifacts."

"Sounds lonely," Connie said.

He looked away because he'd never mentioned Gina to his mother and now wasn't the time or place. He felt oddly possessive of Gina, as if she were his little shining treasure, and he didn't want to play twenty questions about her—especially with his mother.

Lois said, "Well, summer in North Carolina is full of sudden rainstorms. Don't drive down if the weather's really bad."

"There's no way to communicate if he gets stuck up there," Connie said to Lois. "No phone or cell service. I don't like that."

"Mom, I'll be fine. Just know that if I don't come home, I'm stranded at the professor's house."

"Better to be safe than sorry," Lois warned.

"I still don't like it," Connie grumbled.

Drake excused himself and went to his room, where he lay on his bed daydreaming of holding Gina, of kissing her, of touching her, until his mom called him to supper.

Drake passed the summer happier than he'd ever been in his life. That was Gina's doing. She met him at the gate each morning, spent most mornings in the same room with him doing needlework or reading. They often ate lunch in the gardens, surrounded by butterflies and the scent of roses. He held her hand, sometimes afraid to blink lest she vanish like a dream. In the afternoons she went upstairs and played the piano or danced. He heard the music above him, her piano ever solemn, her crazy Victor machine tinny and far away. More than anything, Drake longed to kiss her. He lacked the courage to try.

He left at four, when the old clock chimed. And he arrived home at four, which made no sense. And yet the clock chimed regularly throughout the day, as if it knew each hour intimately and kept each one perfectly. He itched to inspect the clock more closely, but he never went near it. He'd learned his lesson the day Dennison had shouted that the clock was off-limits.

From time to time Dennison would drift into the workroom, scan Drake's paperwork, nod and say, "Good work. Carry on." Drake hadn't been paid yet, but he felt he'd probably get a lump sum at the end of the summer. He just couldn't bring up the money now.

One afternoon the professor didn't leave the room. He rocked back on his heels, cleared his throat.

Drake looked up. "Something else you want?"

"Gina's fond of you," Dennison said bluntly.

Drake felt tension tighten like a knot inside him. "I like her."

"She's"—Dennison halted, searching for a word, finished with—"inexperienced."

Drake's antenna went up. What was the professor trying to say?

Dennison put his hands behind his back, looked up. "Be good to her," he said quietly, and left the room.

Drake went numb. How else could he be to a girl like Gina?

On Saturday, Drake stopped and bought a cheap watch. Normally he used his cell for keeping time, but none of its functions ever worked at the Dennisons' house. His cell worked going to the old house and it worked once he left the property, but not while he was on the property. The old grandfather clock kept time, but in a fashion Drake couldn't figure out.

The next morning, he parked, checked the watch and saw the second hand sweeping the face and keeping the time perfectly. Now that he was familiar with the curves of the mountain, it only took thirty-five minutes to drive up Sandstone. He stuffed the watch into his pocket.

Before meeting Gina at the gate, he checked the new watch. Only five minutes had passed, which he figured was how long it took him to limp up the slight hill and round the bend on the path. Later, when he was alone working and before Gina slipped into the room with her sewing, he pulled the watch from his pocket. The second hand no longer moved and the hands were stopped. He stared, unable to believe it had quit working. He shook it hard, but the hands stayed stationary. In the hall, the old grandfather clock struck ten. His nerves coiled. What was going on?

Just then Gina entered the room and Drake shoved the watch back into his pocket. She smiled at him and took her chair by the window. "You all right?"

"I'm just fine," Drake answered. "Do I look bad?"

"A little pale," she said.

"Probably the drive up. Lots of twists in the road."

"Would you like some lemonade? That usually helps me feel better."

He shook his head. She came over, touched his forehead. "You feel fine."

Her smile calmed him. Her touch made his heartbeat trip. "Is the clock in the hall correct?"

"I guess so." She walked to her chair. "Why?"

He cast about for a reason that didn't sound wonko. "Um—sometimes it seems to go faster, sometimes slower."

She tipped her head. "I think it's working. I'll ask Father—"

"No. That's okay . . . don't mention it to him. I'm probably just not hearing the chimes correctly. You know, losing count. Or something."

From the hallway, the clock began to chime. "I'll count out loud," Gina said, and proceeded to do so until the chimes stopped at ten. "Ten o'clock," she said, "That seems about right."

Drake swallowed and felt a shiver go up his spine. It had already chimed ten o'clock before she'd walked into the room. They'd been talking. Surely time had moved forward since then. But as Gina bent over her sewing, Drake eased out a deep breath. For some reason, time had stopped, then resumed, allowing more time for him to be with Gina Dennison. He couldn't understand it, or explain it. He decided instead to be grateful for it.

Despite the weirdness of the big clock, Drake knew time was passing. He saw it every day in the way the pile of boxes he moved from the incomplete to the complete stack along the wall. He saw it on the calendar that hung in his mother's kitchen. He felt it in the air—hot July temperatures that fell sticky on his skin gave way to a bit of coolness weeks later. Just as long as he could be with Gina, he was content. He slowed his work on the boxes. He hurried up the mountain every day, longing to be with her. At the end of August school would start and his world would change. He'd be butting up against his peers, kids who would dismiss him because he wasn't like them.

One warm still day, with his heart hammering like a drum, he turned to Gina on the garden bench where they sat finishing lunch and asked, "Can we stay in touch after you go home?"

"I'd like that." She was slicing an apple and placing the juicy slivers on a plate between them.

"You would?" He had wanted the answer she gave but was surprised because it had come quickly, with no hesitancy. Maybe, just maybe, she liked him too.

She laughed. "Of course, silly. You're my friend."

Friend. The word reverberated in his head and sobered him. He didn't want to be only her friend. Screwing up his courage, he said, "I have an idea. Why don't I come up here on Saturday and take you down to the city. We can see a movie. You know, popcorn . . . the whole works. Can we do that?"

Her eyes clouded. "I—I can't. Thank you for inviting me, though."

"Oh." It was as if she'd slammed a door in his face.

He'd misread the signs of togetherness completely. She was lonely. He was her only company. How could he have imagined she hung out with him for any other reason?

"You're my dearest friend," she said.

She'd used the word *friend* again. That sealed it. She felt nothing for him. What girl wanted to be seen in public with a gimp? He pushed himself up from the bench, straightened his bad leg.

She took his arm. "I—I would if I could. But I can't."

He didn't believe her. Girls lied. "It's all right," he said, shaking loose. "Nothing special showing now anyway." He hid his pain with a smile. "Better get back to work."

"Drake, don't go—"

He limped away from her and the overpowering smell of roses. He didn't turn around.

6

His mother took off from work and accompanied Drake for registration and orientation at what would be his new high school. Drake had asked for the morning off too, telling Dennison the day before that he'd come in late. "No need," Dennison told him. "Take the day off. You've earned it."

Drake was closing in on the end of his project, so he could afford to take a day off. After what he saw as Gina's rejection of him, he was having difficulty being around her every day anyway, so when his mother reminded him about registration, Drake was glad for the break. He felt the cold hand of reality clutch him, though, the minute they walked through the high school's doors. For Drake, a kid who wasn't created perfect, school was the unhappiest place on the planet. His unhappiness doubled when he also realized he was a new kid, meaning he had no friends or acquaintances.

"Nice building," his mother said as they followed the registration signs to the gym. "Newer than your school in Ohio."

Big whoop. Kids milled in the halls—freshmen, he assumed. They looked as lost as he felt. He was heading down the hall when a girl came up to him. She was almost as tall as he was, had dark hair, a nice smile and ordinary features. She wore a name tag: BETH, STUDENT GUIDE. She greeted them with "Hey, I'm here to answer any questions. Welcome."

"Where's the gym?" Connie asked.

"This way."

Drake wished his mother hadn't spoken to Beth. How hard could it be to follow signs on their own?

Beth kept pace with Drake to accommodate his slower gait. "You don't look like a freshman. No panic in your eyes."

"I'm a junior. Transferring in."

"Hey, I'll be a junior too. Beth Karondokis, yearbook coordinator, class VP, choir, Green Committee member. I've generally got my fingers in everything that happens around here."

He smiled slightly over her description of herself. She was bubbly and self-assured. He envied her affability. "Drake Iverson."

"My dad owns a Greek pizzeria near the school where all the kids hang. The only Greek pizza place in the city. Actually, the only Greek pizza place in North

Carolina." She made a funny face, forcing a real smile from Drake.

She sent him a sidelong glance as they walked. "CP?"

He felt his body grow rigid. She'd boldly nailed him and his handicap. "Right."

"I have a younger sister with CP," Beth said. "Lisa is much worse off than you. She's a great kid."

Was that supposed to console him? Drake never knew how to deal with any girl, let alone a kind one.

They stopped at the gym's entrance. "We're here. Why don't you go register and then let me give you a guided tour? And when school starts, look me up. I'll intro you around to my friends."

"Go on," his mother said. "I'll wait in the bleachers."

Drake shot her a hostile look. Didn't his mom get that he didn't want to hang around and go on a tour with a girl who probably pitied him?

Beth put her hand on his shoulder. "Get it done and come right back." She leaned closer, gave him an impish grin. "And welcome to the jungle."

"I don't like it when you're mad at me," Gina said from the doorway of Drake's work space.

He looked up. "I'm not mad at you." The truth was, he was hurt.

"You're mad because I wouldn't go to the movie with you."

"I'm over it."

She came to his worktable and turned him to face her. "Believe me, I would have gone with you if it had been possible."

Her eyes were so blue and so sincere that Drake felt his cool resolve begin to melt. When a mist filled her eyes, he came undone. "Look, Gina, I understand that going out with a guy who walks like he's drunk isn't every girl's dream date."

"Is that what you think?"

He heard an edge in her voice. "It's the way it is. I've learned to accept it."

"You know, Drake, you're the only one who thinks of yourself as crippled. I don't see your limp when we're together."

"Hard to believe."

"Hard for me to believe that you don't see what I see when I look at you."

"What do you see, Gina?"

She rose on her tiptoes and kissed his cheek. "I see someone I care about."

She left the room and he stood staring at the space that had held her, desire eating through him like a virus.

The warbling from Gina's music machine kept crashing into Drake's ability to concentrate on his work. The sound grated like fingernails on a blackboard, and for some reason seemed louder than usual even though it was coming down three flights of stairs. Every now and then it slowed, stopped and then speeded up, letting him know that she had wound the crank handle. How could she ever dance tending to that crappy machine every few minutes?

He threw down his paperwork and hobbled to the door. He glanced at the old clock, was surprised to see that it was only two-fifteen. Except for the ticking clock and the tinny music, the house lay silent. He had no idea where Dennison was, but at the moment, he didn't care. Taking a deep breath, Drake crossed the hallway and began a long slow climb up the stairs.

He stood outside the door of the attic room sweating, waiting while his shriveled leg muscle and breathing settled down from the exertion. When he regained control of both, he stepped through the doorway. Gina was pirouetting en pointe, her arms and legs in classic ballet poses. His heart thumped crazily, but not from his climb. She was sheer beauty, as fragile as a flower. Sunlight shot through the windows, and in its beams, tiny flurries of dust rose from the floor as she spun. Her white blond hair was pulled into a severe bun, accentuating her cheekbones and eyes.

She spun so much that Drake grew dizzy watching her. She broke her pose, bounded across the wooden floor, whirling as she leapt. Her athleticism amazed him. There might have been a time when he would have felt intimidated and left wanting, but now he was mesmerized by her skill and beauty. When she finally caught sight of him, she cried, "Drake! What are you doing here?"

He snapped from his trance, felt his color rise. "I, um—I wanted to see you dance."

She came to him, splay-footed because of her toe shoes. Her face was rosy with the glow of exercise, and perspiration stood out on her face and throat. He stared at the throbbing pulse in her neck and wanted to suck it. He snapped his gaze to her eyes. "Do you mind if I watch?"

She laughed. "I haven't danced in front of an audience since I left Boston in the spring."

"Then it's okay?"

"It's okay." She took his hand and led him into the large room.

"Maybe I can wind your music machine so you don't have to stop every time and do it."

Another smile lit her face. "That would be wonderful."

"I could bring a better machine to you. One that runs on batteries. I can pick up a few CDs if you tell me the ones you want."

Her smile turned tender, a little sad. "We'll be going home soon. No need to bother."

His heart wrenched. He didn't want her to ever leave. "I'm sorry," he said, meaning more than he could put into words. Sorry she was leaving. Sorry he'd withdrawn from her.

She touched his arm, ducked her head to meet his eyes. "I know."

With the two words, he knew she'd forgiven him. He

swallowed against a hard knot of emotion clogging his throat.

"I have an idea," she said. She knelt next to a stack of disks in paper sleeves, riffled through them, came up with one and exchanged it for the one on the turntable. She reached for the crank.

"Let me," Drake said. He wound it tight, set the needle on the disk. Voices sang.

"It's my favorite," Gina said. "'Till We Meet Again.'"

The music was scratchy, the beat slow and the words sentimental. He'd never heard the song before and he didn't think much of it, but if Gina liked it . . .

She slipped her arms around him. "Dance with me."

He drew back, shocked by what she was asking. "I can't dance."

"Of course you can."

Looking into her intense blue eyes, he believed her. "I—I'm clumsy."

"I don't care."

His arms went around her and she snuggled against his chest. They swayed together, their bodies touching, his body aching with need and longing for her. She raised her chin and he bent his head and kissed her.

7

Kissing Gina. Drake revisited the moments over and over in his head that weekend. He'd heard dopey love songs telling of "sweet kisses." Lame. But remarkably true. Gina tasted of apples and sugar, and the taste lingered in his mouth.

Drake couldn't get over how different she was from other girls. At school, the popular girls traveled in packs, like show dogs strutting before panels of judges, always on display. Their clothes shouted "Look at me." Their hair was usually a perfected snarl of messiness and their lips pouted with thick layers of shimmering gloss. They giggled, talked loudly enough to draw constant attention to themselves and hung like ornaments on the arms of the guys they liked. Less popular girls were often quieter, moving like shadows in the halls, not flamboyant, but aloof, worshiping from afar the others, male and female, the ones who owned the limelight.

The outsider girls strutted the halls, brimming with attitude. The pecking order was vicious. He recalled a day when he stared a little too long at one girl with spiked purple hair. She'd turned and snapped, "What are you looking at, gimp?"

Gina was like none of them. She was sweet and never talked down to him. She treated him as if he were an important person instead of a tall clumsy boy with a shriveled leg. He found her intoxicating. He didn't want summer to end. He wanted to be with her for all time.

He was grilling burgers on the patio one Sunday afternoon while his mother sliced tomatoes onto a plate at their picnic table. She looked over at Drake and said, "You look happy."

He sent her a sidelong glance. "Why do you say that?"

"You just do."

"Gee, let me wipe it off my face."

"Don't be sarcastic. Happy looks good on you."

He shrugged self-consciously.

Connie spread the tomatoes in a semicircle on the plate and opened a jar of pickles. "I'm your mother. I know when something's up with you." She paused, cocked her head. "Are you in love?"

Drake almost dropped his spatula. He felt his face redden. "What are you saying?"

Connie walked over, her arms crossed with a knowing smile on her face. "I'm right, aren't I?"

He waved her away. "I don't know what you're talking about."

"It's not a bad thing, son. Nothing to be ashamed of. I'm just wondering why you didn't tell me that you've met someone. Talk to me."

He took a deep breath, knowing that she'd eventually wheedle the information out of him. "Okay . . . so I know a girl. She's the professor's daughter."

"Why didn't you tell me?"

"Nothing to tell. Her name's Gina and . . . and she's nice." He was uncomfortably warm. He probably should have mentioned Gina to his mom before now, but he hadn't. Keeping Gina to himself had been self-protective at first. No use talking about what he couldn't have. But now, after holding her and kissing her, he felt she was somehow a part of him.

"Am I going to meet her?"

He thought about Gina's reaction when he'd asked her on a date. She'd said, "I can't." Maybe now she would. "I don't know. They're going back to Boston after Labor Day." School would start for him in a week. He wrapped up his job soon.

"Oh," his mother said, looking disappointed. "I'd really like to meet her."

"I'm going to see her as much as I can until they leave," he said. "I'll try and bring her by for a visit." He was taking a chance—he had no idea whether she'd come.

"She must be special if you like her," Connie said.

What was special was that she liked him, but he didn't say that to his mother. He scooped up the burgers and put them on a plate. "Dinner," he announced instead.

Drake had noticed that although it remained hot in the city at the foot of the mountain, the air was growing cooler on Sandstone. On his drive up in the mornings, he saw hints of autumn color in the foliage, saw berries on bushes turning red and birds beginning to flock together for long flights to sunnier climates. Fall was coming—everywhere except at 13 Sandstone Mountain.

"You must be a heck of a gardener," Drake said to Gina one afternoon. They were holding hands, walking the path that wandered between flowerbeds.

"Why do you say that?"

"Because these flowers look just the same as when I first came to apply for my job." He paused on the path. "Like these." He gently shook a pink mop-head hydrangea.

"Oh, they'll die when it gets colder."

"You mean without you to take care of them." Drake looked over the gardens, at roses still full and bright, at black-eyed Susans standing tall and summery, at tulips still holding on to their waxy spring petals.

Gina turned to face him, slipped her arms around his

waist. "Are we out here to talk about flowers? Or do you want to kiss me?"

He grinned, bent toward her lips. "What flowers?"

Drake made his way along the crowded hall on the first day of school. He hugged the wall, not wanting to become entangled in the swarm of foot traffic. His mood was dark because the last time he'd seen Gina, they'd argued. His mother was on his case about meeting Gina, but nothing he said could persuade her to come down the mountain with him. He'd become so frustrated with her refusals that he'd made her cry. Now he only felt miserable, because Gina had hurt him all over again, and he'd said things to hurt her.

"Hey, Drake!"

Surprised, he turned and saw a dark-haired girl weaving through the mass of bodies toward him. She skidded to a stop. "It's me—Beth," she said with a breathless smile. "You know, your faithful guide."

She clicked into place in his head. Beth from registration day. "Hi."

"Crazy, isn't it? First week is wild . . . everybody trying to find their way."

"I take my time," he said.

"So let me see your class card."

He pulled out the card and she quickly scanned it. "We have third-period trig together. That's cool."

"Sure," he said, not meaning it. He realized she might honestly be a nice person, but he didn't care about anything except Gina right now.

"Our lunch periods overlap too. Look for me when you hit the cafeteria and I'll intro you around to my posse."

He didn't crack a smile. His mind was truly elsewhere.

She leaned in. "Get it? Posse? Friends?"

"I get it. That's fine." He was not quite rude. Beth was trying to make him feel welcome. "I'll look for you," he said, with an apologetic shrug. "I had a tough weekend. I'm a bit out of it."

"No prob," Beth said.

"Guess I'd better get to first period." The human traffic crunch had thinned and Drake pushed off from the wall.

"I'll walk with you," Beth said.

"I'll just slow you down. Make you late."

"Like that's never happened," she said, rolling her eyes. "This way."

They walked in silence, Drake ever mindful of his bad leg and wounded heart.

8

Drake stayed away from Gina as long as he could—thirty-six hours. When school let out on the first day, he called his mother and said he was going up to the Dennisons'. Once there, Drake stood at the gate staring at the house and gathering his courage. The stones looked a little dingy, and the lawn, so beautiful days before, now looked brown, as if it were drying up and withering.

He looked skyward and saw dark clouds gathering, heard a rumble of distant thunder. A storm was coming. When he knocked on the front door, Gina flung it open. She looked terrified. She hurled herself at Drake, almost knocking him over. Alarmed, he held her. "What's wrong?"

"It's going to storm and Father's not here." She pulled Drake into the house.

The foyer had a hollow sound. Furniture was covered with sheets and blankets in rooms off the foyer. Drake's workroom had been emptied of boxes and books. She was really leaving. He held her more tightly. "I'll stay with you." He forgot all about their argument.

"Don't leave me."

"Not happening."

The great grandfather clock still stood in the hall, its hands frozen at four o'clock. Drake knew it had to be close to five, because when he had parked the car, his cell had displayed four-thirty-five. He didn't have to look at his phone to know it wasn't functioning, because it never worked on the premises.

"Do you mind if we go up to my studio?" Her eyes looked frightened.

"If we go slow."

They took their time up the stairs, arriving just as thunder clapped and rain pelted the windows. Gina cried out, began to tremble.

"It's just rain," Drake said, trying to soothe her, not understanding her irrational fears. "And we're safe here inside." He stroked her hair, walked her to the sofa. A great bolt of lightning split the sky, cracking like a whip. Gina screamed. He took her in his arms. "It's okay. I'm with you."

The room was dusky gray and growing darker. "Look, I'll light all your candles," Drake said, in an attempt to quell her terror.

She clutched him tighter. "Don't go."

"It'll be all right." He pried her arms away, found

matches near the record machine and hobbled around the room lighting every wick, until the room glowed like a curtain holding off the dark. When he returned, she huddled in his arms.

"You won't leave me?"

"No way." He kissed her.

She pressed closer, clinging to his mouth. Together they tumbled onto the sofa, exploring one another's bodies with mouths and hands. He kissed her throat, sweet-salty from her fear. He pulled aside the neckline of her blouse, heard her moan, and ventured to taste the swell of her breast. She reached for his hand, brought his palm to her breast, and he felt the hammer of her heart, heard the sound of her breath coming in short gasps. Heat seeped through his clothes, and all he wanted was to feel her body on his, skin to skin.

He burned and ached with a primal need as old as time. The need was feral, mind-bending. He'd never experienced it before. He was losing control. "Gina, what if . . . what if your dad shows up?"

"He can't get back," she whispered, tugging Drake's shirt out of his jeans.

"Why? Where did he go?" By now Drake knew the rain had made it impossible for either him or the professor to get up or down the mountain.

Her hands stroked his bare skin. He thought he'd spontaneously combust.

"It's raining," she said. "He can't get through the static."

Through what static? his last vestige of logic asked.

"Do you love me?" she asked.

"I love you," he answered, forgetting all else as the vortex of passion sucked him into ecstasy.

It rained solidly for two days. He thought about his mother. She'd be worried, maybe frantic about his safety. He had no way to reach her and tell her he was all right. But she knew where he was. When he did get home there would be hell to pay, but now, in these hours with Gina, he didn't care.

The house was without electricity from the storm, and the rain fell steadily outside. Gina lit candles, carried one with them through the darkened house wherever they went, while the halo of light threw their shadows on the walls like wandering ghosts. They foraged for food in the kitchen, made meals of apples, cheese, some stale bread. "We don't have much," she explained. "Pretty well cleaned out the icebox a few days ago."

Drake nibbled on her ear, making her giggle. "I've got all I need."

They slept on an oversized couch in one of the rooms downstairs, wound tightly in each other's arms, using blankets that had covered furniture. The first night Drake slept restlessly to the relentless drumming of rain on the roof, the whip of wind rattling window glass, the distant roll of thunder. The next night he slept more soundly, found comfort in the beat of the rain and the feel of Gina spooned up against his chest. He awoke with a vague feeling that something was missing. As night turned to soggy dawn he finally locked onto what it was—the clock. It chimed no more. Maybe he should wind it. Gina would know where her father kept the key.

The patter of rain slowed. He kissed the back of Gina's warm neck. "Wake up. I think the sun's going to shine today."

She moaned, turned over. "My head hurts," she whispered.

Drake pulled back, lit a candle, held it toward her. Her lips looked parched and her skin had gone pale except for two dots of hot pink color on her cheekbones. He pressed his cheek to her forehead. "You feel hot. Maybe it's too many covers." He kicked off the blankets. Chill hit his skin.

Gina moaned. "I can't move. Everything hurts."

"Do you have some aspirin?"

"Don't know," she mumbled.

He pulled himself off the couch, covered Gina with the blanket and struggled into his clothes. "I'll look around."

"Don't . . . leave . . ."

"I bet you have a fever. I need to find some aspirin."

He hobbled off, rummaged through kitchen cupboards, went upstairs, searched medicine cabinets. Everything was empty. He started to panic. If Gina was really sick, what was he going to do? Back downstairs, he found

a cloth, wet it and pressed it to her fiery forehead. She
coughed. He heard rattling in her chest. What was happening? How could she have become so sick overnight?
Fear squeezed his stomach. He said, "Come on, honey.
We have to get down the mountain. You need a doctor."

"No . . ." With pitiful weakness, she pushed against
him. "Can't . . . go. Wait for Father."

"I have a car," Drake said, as if talking to a truculent
child. "We'll leave your dad a note." He'd take her home
to his mother; she'd know what to do.

He sat her up, fed her arms into her robe, slid her feet
into slippers. He wrapped her arm over his neck, gripped
her waist and shuffled her toward the front door. She was
deadweight. He encouraged her outside, down the porch
steps, onto the front lawn. He was sweating, his breath
heaving, his legs trembling. He cursed his bad leg. He had
to get her to his car, and there was a long way to go and
rough muddy terrain to get through. Without warning,
rain began again. It fell hard, coming in cool waves. Gina
cried out in pain.

"Just a little more," he told her. "Hang on."

He was almost to the gate when behind him, he heard
the word "Stop!"

Drake glanced over his shoulder and saw Dennison
seemingly coming out of nowhere. He ran toward them.

"She's sick," Drake shouted above the rain. "We need
to get her to a doctor." Weak with relief, Drake held up
at the gate. Dennison would help them.

Dennison reached out, pulled Gina from Drake's arms, shifted her weight toward himself. "Go!" Dennison said. Rain poured down his face in rivulets.

"We just have to get her to my car!"

"She's not going anywhere. She's staying here with me."

"No!" Drake lurched toward the man. "Don't you get it? She's sick! We have to find a doctor."

"Get out!" Dennison lifted a limp rain-drenched Gina and carried her back toward the house.

Stunned, Drake started after him, but his bad leg slid in the mud and he fell to his knees.

Dennison turned, yelled, "Leave. I'll handle it. She's my child."

Drake reached for the gate behind him, hauled himself upright. "She's got to have a doctor!" he cried. "Let me help her."

Dennison shuffled backward. "Go," he commanded once more. He paused. "Listen, there's a large rock on the back corner of the property. Look for it later," he added enigmatically.

Drake watched helplessly as Dennison carried Gina through the pouring rain, up the porch steps and into the house.

9

Drake flung open the front door, shouted, "Mom! I need your help!" The rain had stopped by the time he'd come off the mountain and headed across town. He was soaking wet and shivering uncontrollably.

His mother ran from the kitchen. "What's wrong? Honey, what's the matter?"

"Gina's sick and I can't get her father to take her to a doctor."

Connie stopped short. "Drake, I'm sorry—"

He butted in with, "I'm sorry about being gone for two days. I—I couldn't get off Sandstone because of the rain."

She stared at him. "What are you talking about? You've only been gone a few hours. I'm in the middle of fixing supper for us."

His mind reeled. "No . . . I've been with Gina for two days."

"Stop it. You're scaring me. You left here right after school. Now it's almost six."

He braced his hand on a wall, suddenly light-headed.

Connie rushed closer. "You're soaked to the bone."

"Dennison took Gina away from me. I wanted to bring her here . . . to a doctor."

"He's her father. He'll take her to a doctor himself."

"No . . . I couldn't help her. My leg . . ." Drake felt as if he were swimming through fog.

Connie reached up and touched his forehead. "Good Lord! You're burning up!"

"You don't get it. It's Gina. She's really sick." His words felt thick in his sore throat. His head hurt. He went woozy and his legs buckled.

Connie caught his arm, grabbed her car keys from the catchall table in the foyer. "Get in my car," she commanded. "We're going to the ER. And I mean right now."

"But Gina—"

"You're the one who's sick."

Drake was hardly aware of the ride to the ER. He shivered violently the whole way, and once there, seemed to be immediately taken into the triage area. A nurse covered him with warmed blankets, took his temperature and blood pressure. He heard the nurse tell his mother, "I'll get the doctor."

Other hands probed him, felt his limbs; something scraped the back of his throat. "Gina . . . ," Drake whispered. "Help her."

A man's voice said, ". . . need to check him in."

Drake said, "No."

The man's voice said, "Get him up to ICU isolation."

Connie asked, "What's wrong?"

"We'll run some tests, but whatever it is, he's a very sick boy."

Drake tried to move but couldn't. As the gurney beneath him began to roll, he fell into blackness.

Dreams fought with reality in Drake's mind. He felt needle pricks and saw people wearing masks bending over him. He drifted into his workroom on Sandstone Mountain, saw Gina sitting beside the sunny window, creating rows of purple flowers on squares of linen. She would look up and smile; then her image quivered like heat waves on a distant road as Drake reached for her, and she melted away. He felt a mask fitted over his nose and mouth, heard a machine beeping next to a bed—his bed? He wasn't sure. He saw Dennison through a veil of rain, and when Drake tried to force his way through it, his feet became cemented to the ground and he couldn't move. He saw his mother's eyes peering at him, her hair covered with a head scarf, her mouth and chin swathed in a green mask. He felt hot and cold, and his body ached as if a truck had run him over.

Reality won out, coming into focus for Drake four days after he was admitted to ICU. His doctor introduced himself one early morning during rounds. "Dr. Sherman," he told Drake.

"What happened?"

"Flu," Sherman said, adjusting Drake's oxygen mask. "H1N1 variety. You had a bad case, and we threw every antibiotic in our arsenal at it."

"Swine flu?"

"A misnomer. Its DNA harkens back to the pandemic of 1918." Sherman wrote on Drake's chart as he spoke. "Soldiers brought it with them from Europe, unknowingly infecting people. The virus spread like wildfire worldwide. The pandemic killed maybe one hundred million people. The current strain isn't as deadly, but still plenty of people have died from it, mostly the young. We've haven't figured out why. Your mother says you didn't get the vaccine for it."

Drake flicked his eyes toward the door. "Where—?"

"She went home to shower and change, said she'd return in an hour. She's been here round the clock."

"When can I go home?"

"Couple of more days."

Drake's heart sank. How was Gina? How could he find out?

"Mom, I'm begging you to do this for me." Drake lifted his oxygen mask to speak clearly.

"Drake, please forget about this girl for a while. I'm sure her father's taken care of her."

"But I have to know!"

Connie repositioned the mask on his face. Drake wanted to rip it off and throw it on the floor.

"One of your new friends from school called to check on you." His mother tried to change the subject.

What friend? Drake had no friends except Gina.

"Her name was Beth. Isn't that the girl who showed you around at registration?"

Drake waved his mother's words away. "Mom, please go up and check on Gina. It's the only way. I'll draw you a map of how to get there. Please!"

Her shoulders sagged. "Is she that important to you?"

"Yes."

She pinched the bridge of her nose. "I'll ask my friend Lois to ride up with me tomorrow after work."

"There were so many trees across the road on Sandstone Mountain, we couldn't even get close to number thirteen."

Drake's stomach knotted with his mother's report. Lois had come into his room with her and nodded repeatedly to second the bad news. "Did you try?"

"A cat couldn't have gotten through that mess of trees. They were lying every which way, pines and oaks. It was a real mess."

Drake turned his head, shoved his partially eaten dinner away from him on the rolling table a nurse had placed across his bed. He had no appetite. All he wanted was to get out of this hole.

Connie stopped the tray from sliding onto the floor. "Now listen up, son. I know you've been sick and I know you're worried about this Gina, but I won't excuse bad manners. Lois gave up her afternoon to go on this little jaunt with me, so yes, we tried and couldn't get there."

Lois cleared her throat, stepped between Drake's hospital bed and Connie. "You know, my mother was born and raised in this city. She's eighty-three now, and she's a real historian about these parts of North Carolina. Used to be a docent in the museum downtown, and can rattle off information about the area all the way from before the Civil War."

Drake sighed, bored.

Lois forged ahead. "Anyway, I asked her about Sandstone and the families who used to live up there. A few of those houses have been passed down from generation to generation. You know, before developers came in and started buying up properties and building new vacation homes."

"And?" Drake said, to keep Lois on message.

"Well, she recalls that back after the war ended, in 'forty-four, a professor from some fancy university in Boston moved into the old McCaw residence. Pity they had to sell out back then, but they lost both sons in the war." She shrugged her plump shoulders. "So this old man was a recluse. Didn't have anything to do with anybody. Wouldn't let anyone on his property except the grocery delivery boy. In those days, there was a store at the foot of the mountain and they'd bring orders up to you. Not like today."

Drake was growing impatient listening to Lois ramble. "What happened to him? Did he have a daughter?"

"No kin. Just him. Mama said the house burned down in the mid-fifties, and the old man died in the fire."

Drake gritted his teeth. He was over hearing Lois's meaningless story.

Connie asked, "What happened to the house?"

"Don't know," Lois said.

Exasperated, Drake sank into the pillow. He didn't know one thing more about Gina than he had the day he'd gotten sick.

Drake was cleared to return to school, and Connie sent him off with a list of Mother's dos and don'ts. As soon as he was in his car, he ditched school and headed up Sandstone. The higher up he drove, the more he saw the colors of autumn. He remembered once hearing "Spring marches up the mountain, autumn flows down it." He understood the meaning now. Bright red and orange leaves exploded on tree limbs. In the valley, where he lived, the trees were barely tinged with color. Overhead the sky was brilliant blue, and the air was so clear and clean it stung his lungs.

The road veering off to the Dennisons' was littered with leaves and branches. No wonder his mother hadn't been able to get there. He ended up parking far from his original summer space and making a slow laborious climb over felled rotting trees. They looked as if they'd been there for years instead of only a few weeks.

By the time he reached the bend in the path to the Dennisons' property, his bad leg ached and his lungs burned, but his longing for Gina drove him beyond his pain. He caught his breath, straightened, rounded the bend. He stopped cold. In front of him lay the property and the grand old house in ruins.

10

✧

Drake went numb with shock. The house lay broken, wooden walls ripped and charred down to the stone walls black with soot. The roof was completely caved in, the turret looking as if some giant's hand had clawed it apart. The white picket fence where Gina met him every day was gray with age, the paint chipped and peeling, sections of it lying on the ground. The wisteria vine was so overgrown he would have needed a machete to get through it.

Drake limped toward the broken hulk of what had once been Gina's beautiful home, stepped over a section of the downed fence, plowed his way through overgrown weeds that only weeks before had been a lush green lawn. Maybe he was going crazy. Maybe his summer job had never happened. Maybe everything had been an illusion—the work and Gina, Gina, Gina.

He stopped in front of the cracked and broken porch,

now impossible to navigate. Lizards rustled over burned boards and small animals scurried out of his way. Dazed, Drake heard Lois's words: ". . . burned to the ground in the mid-fifties."

And then he remembered the last thing Dennison had said to him before taking Gina back into the house. "There's a large rock on the back corner of the property. Look for it later." It had made no sense. And yet . . .

Drake took his time walking beside the ruined house along what had been the path he'd taken into the gardens. There were no gardens now, just weeds and brush, dead growths that he couldn't recognize as ever having been flowers. He found tangles of thorny rosebushes, all dead. He passed the weathered bench where he and Gina had sat for summer lunches and stolen kisses. A fist-sized lump clogged his throat.

The back line of the property was semicircular, with the largest area marked by tree stumps and a sheer drop into autumn-colored woods. He hiked the long perimeter, his leg in spasms. In a far back corner, Drake found a wedge of jutting stone. It stood a good four feet high and held faded charcoal markings in the shape of an arrowhead, pointing down. Goose bumps skittered up his back. He'd handled a lot of arrowheads during his summer job. Someone had left him a message.

He searched the ground for a sturdy stick, found one and began to poke the area surrounding the rock. Nothing. "Deeper," he told himself. With two hands, he shoved the stick hard into layers of dead leaves and dirt. The stick hit something solid. More rock? Drake shifted awkwardly to his knees and dug through the rotting wet foliage with his bare hands. He touched the surface of something hard and smooth. With the stick he pried a rusty metal box from the earth.

He scraped dirt off the top, saw that it was the old square breadbox that had once sat on the Dennisons' kitchen counter. With shaking hands Drake hammered the stuck lid off with a nearby stone. Inside was Gina's sewing kit, musty-smelling, brittle with moisture. There was also a long envelope, better preserved because it had been wrapped in a thick layer of plastic wrap. He stroked the sewing basket, unable for the moment to open it. Instead he unwrapped the envelope and with cold dirt-covered fingers unsealed it. The words were written in Dennison's distinctive flowing handwriting. Drake sat in the old leaves, leaned up against the big rock and read.

SEPTEMBER 1952

I hope Drake Iverson is reading this, because it's meant for him and will make no sense to anyone else. I have much to explain to you, Drake. Explanations you deserve. Where to begin?

The clock, I guess. You were always suspicious of it— with good reason. I found it in an old attic in Boston in 1917 and quickly learned it was a time portal.

Drake stopped, reread the last sentence. Time portal? Was the professor joking? Making an excuse for taking Gina away? And yet Drake had to admit that the clock had been weird—beyond weird.

I do not know if it was created in the past or the future; I only know that it allowed me and Gina to travel through time. In 1917, World War I broke out, and in 1918 a virulent influenza began to spread around the world and kill more people than the war itself. I sought to save my precious Regina from this disease.

Drake paused. Gina had been real. All that had happened to them had been real. And the "days" he'd spent holding her, loving her, had also happened, with mere hours stretched somehow by the clock's bending of time.

I cannot tell you why I chose to bring her forward to this time period. Perhaps I simply thought that science had advanced enough so that she would be safe. We first came one year ago for the summer, but she was desperately lonely. When we came this year, I advertised for a summer helper, a companion for her, really. When you came, when the portal that extended outward to the white fence allowed you inside its boundaries, I was overjoyed. I had no inkling that it would. That Gina liked you instantly was even better. Your curiosity about the clock almost destroyed things, but you stayed in spite of my dire warnings and you did your job, and yes, you loved my daughter. I wasn't blind to your feelings, my boy—or to Gina's. I passed through the portal daily, returning to Harvard—I really was a professor there, with summer classes to teach.

There was a flaw with the portal, however. While it allowed the future to come into our world, it did not allow the past to leave its protection. We learned this the hard way when Gina's cat left the property one day and turned to ashes and dust in front of our eyes. Horrifying. And that is why I could not allow you to carry Gina off the property for medical treatment that night. She would have evaporated in your arms.

Drake shuddered, thinking how close he'd come to destroying Gina. He shivered against the autumn chill, glanced at his cell phone, now working perfectly. Although it was practically noon, the sunlight offered no warmth.

The clock had flaws, which I had neither the expertise nor the skill to repair. Storms caused the portal to become unstable. It warped ahead or backward or stopped working altogether. Electrical static made it impossible to pass from one time period to the other. Now you know why Gina was so terrified of the thunder and lightning. If I was stuck in our time, she had to wait alone, trapped in a universe she couldn't escape or understand. As for you, nothing from your era—your phone, your computer—could function within the protected halo of the portal because these items had not been yet invented. And yet the portal allowed you to pass through. I know not why. Nor could I ask any of the scientific minds at Harvard, who would take it for advanced study. A time portal was far too dangerous a tool to fall into hands that could misuse its power.

I returned Gina to 1919, where she died from the flu.

Drake's vision blurred and he stopped reading. She was gone . . . very close to a hundred years gone. But he had held her, kissed her, loved her. And she'd taken his heart with her.

One day when you are older, and if you ever travel to Boston, here is the place where she is buried.

Again Drake stopped reading, all but blinded with tears. He vowed to go to the address Dennison provided and visit Gina's grave one day. He took a shaky breath and returned to reading the letter.

As for me, well, I hardly matter. My grief was fathomless, and I had no reason to return to this time period. So I remained in my own time, lived my days as best I could. I escaped the flu (how ironic that I should live and she should die). I retired from teaching when World War II broke out. Another war! Do men ever learn? I came here in the late forties, bought the house and property. I have left it in a trust to Harvard, which assuredly doesn't realize they own it, for few people check out these things.

I know one day you will come here seeking answers, and I hope you will discover this message and Gina's sewing basket. Inside, I've also left you some money, as I know I never paid you for your work. Remember the bills were minted in the early fifties, and that makes them more valuable than the money of your time.

One more thing, Drake . . . I have destroyed the clock, so the time portal is no more. No one needs to time-travel into heartbreak. I leave you with a final comfort: your name was the last word on Gina's lips.

Regards,
Dr. Avery Dennison

11

Drake sat staring at the back side of the destroyed house and at the gardens, holding the letter detailing answers to questions he could never share. Time travel. Who would believe him? He thought about his case of the flu, and of Gina's. Of how sick she'd been and how she'd probably suffered. He lived in a time when the science of medicine had been far enough advanced to help him. She had not. Her flu had morphed into his variety, and he had been saved. His leg cramped from being curled under him and his back ached from leaning against the hard rock. Yet he couldn't leave. He picked up the sewing basket, held it in his lap, feeling the weight of it, the reality of it. Gina had touched it.

He lifted the lid, saw two envelopes, one holding money, the other a neatly folded handkerchief. The material had yellowed with age, but a nosegay of purple lilacs graced one corner. A note was fastened to the cloth with a straight pin. In Gina's hand, he read:

In the Victorian love language of flowers, purple is what is given when the first emotions of love stir in one's heart. I give you this, dear Drake, to express what is blooming in my heart even now as we sit together in the workroom. I wish you saw yourself as I see you— strong and handsome, with a smile that makes me weak. You fret about an imperfect leg and fail to see your perfect heart. All my love—Gina

Drake buried his face in the handkerchief, and although it was very old he could still inhale the rosewater scent of her. "I love you," he whispered.

Drake staggered upright, shook out his bad leg, waited for the cramping to ease. He tucked Dennison's letter into the basket, kept the handkerchief in his hand. Having known and loved Gina meant that his life would never be the same; he was already old beyond his years. Love could do that. The thought made him smile.

He thought about the mountain, the ground where he stood, about the people who'd lived here so long ago. He'd touched their artifacts, the tangible proof of their existence. They were all travelers through time, each of them bound to it, like it or not. In the city below he had a life waiting for him. He would finish high school and college and become an architect. And he would build a great house like the one in front of him had once been. Then and there he swore an oath to do it. Gina had made him understand his own worth.

Cradling the basket, Drake started the long, difficult trek to his car. A hawk's cry forced him to look skyward. The bird swooped and soared, sunlight sifting through its feathered wings as they caught a draft of wind, lifting it ever higher into the sky.

The Mysteries of Chance

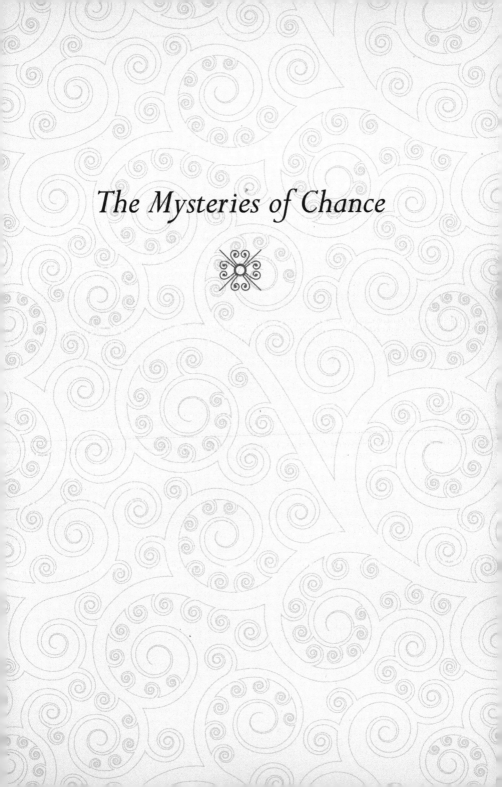

Our love is frozen in time
I'll be your champion and you will be mine . . .

—AMY GRANT, GARY CHAPMAN, KEITH THOMAS

1

She materialized in broad daylight onto a green lawn in front of a brick house on a residential street. She could have handled the mistake easily if the teenage boy across the street hadn't glanced up from washing his car at that very moment. Staring, he dropped the hose. She panicked. This should have never happened. She shouldn't have been seen. The laws governing time travel forbade it.

She crouched, as if making herself smaller would make a difference. It didn't. The boy walked to the end of his driveway, his gaze razoring in on her. He jogged across the street. Maura did the only thing her fifteen-year-old brain could think of—she pretended to pass out.

He leaned over her, blocking the sun and creating a shadow. "Hey, you all right?"

She willed the ground to swallow her.

He dropped to his knees beside her. "You okay?"

She continued her charade.

She heard the alarm in his voice. "I'll call nine-one-one."

She didn't know what 911 was, but what if it drew a crowd? Maura's eyes blinked open. She groaned.

"You came out of nowhere and passed out cold. I should call an ambulance."

Thinking fast, she offered him her hand. She spoke seven languages, was glad he had spoken to her in English, her first. His cadence and dialect sounded odd to her, but she thought she could approximate it if she tried. "Help up," she said.

He tugged her into a sitting position. "Where the heck did you come from? I looked over and the lawn was empty, then *poof!* there you were. Out of thin air."

She rubbed the back of her head, as if she'd struck it when she fell. "Exercising," she said lamely. "You were . . . busy. I came around the corner. I tripped and fell. You looked up when it happened . . . saw me."

"I know what I saw. Empty lawn. Girl on lawn. No trip."

She shrugged, tried to look clueless.

"What's this?" He picked up the handheld device she'd used to transport herself, the forbidden device she'd taken. She wasn't an authorized time traveler. She'd gone into the university's science lab seeking one of her professors, and the device had been sitting on an empty desk. Careless of someone. Time-travel devices were supposed to be kept under lock and key. Hers was a crime of chance. She had picked up the instrument, played with it, figured out its workings; then she had pushed a red button and it had discharged. And she'd landed—where? She had no idea. She only knew that she was in the past. Would the time police believe her when they came for her?

She eased the device from the boy's hand. "Keeps track of my medical stats." She made up the explanation on the spot.

"Are you sick?"

She needed to get away; needed time to think. "Medical testing."

"You don't look sick. Who are you?" She pressed her lips together, edged away. If the police materialized, if they discovered where she'd landed, if they knew she'd made contact, they would bind the boy, maybe even wipe his mind. "Maura. That's my name."

"Dylan Sorenson," he said.

"I need to go." She stood.

He steadied her. "Where're you going? Did you bump your head?"

"I'm fine." She inched backward.

"Hey, don't run off." He made a grab for her arm. "Someone should check you out. My mom's just across the street. Come let her take a look at you."

"Not now. I'm late." A choke hold of panic tightened her throat. She evaded his grasp, turned and took off. "Catch you later." Maura knew she could outrun him. She

was in her prime, and no one born in the past was as physically advanced as people from her era.

Once she rounded the corner, she looked over her
shoulder to see if he was following. He wasn't. She
slowed, caught her breath. The sun shone brilliantly.
Green grass spread in front of every house as far down
the sidewalk as she could see. Water, thrown by a spin-
ning wand, sparkled on blades of several grassy patches.

She thought the time period beautiful, and as long as
she was here, she figured she'd check it out until the time
cops picked her up. If she didn't disturb anything, what
could it hurt?

Even if she returned instantly, she'd be in serious trouble. But she didn't want to go back. Not yet. She was
eager to explore this society. Until she was ready to leave,
where could she hide?

She walked, attempting to get an idea of where and *when*
she'd landed. In Maura's world, scientists knew that time
was a stream, fluid and ever moving. Time travel plopped
a person into the stream at random if the traveler hadn't
specified time and place. And Maura hadn't planned this
trip.

The neighborhood lawns gave way to streets with
buildings. Traffic began to pass her, cars that rode on noisy
tires instead of a quiet whoosh of compressed air. No
parking on the fringes of a town or city and coming into
the main commercial area on foot or on transport

vehicles. People passed her too, seeming not to notice her, although she was dressed in a body-hugging jumpsuit, a single piece, the high-tech material cool in warm weather, warm in cold weather. By the looks of the trees and flower beds, she figured it was late spring or early summer. She'd heard that the past had been ugly and toxic, but this place didn't seem too bad in spite of the exhaust fumes that made her feel nauseated.

Maura stopped suddenly in front of a building. A sign read CLARKSVILLE PUBLIC LIBRARY, EAST BRANCH. A library. She'd read about such places. They had been storehouses of knowledge at one time. Not like in her day, when anyone could plug into the Intercontinental Information Airstream, or IIA, anytime, anyplace. Maura was relieved by her good fortune. Here was a building that housed present and past, a place where she could learn what was necessary to help her blend in. She bounded up the steps, eager to get started.

By the time night came, Maura was again outside, looking for food and a place to sleep. She wandered back down the streets where she'd first emerged from the time stream. The little houses looked homey and the lawns well kept in this Tennessee city one hundred seventeen years in the past. She wasn't nearly as afraid of discovery by time cops as she had been before her afternoon in the library. The current culture ran on electrically generated energy, so the electromagnetic fields shielded her with static, which acted as a safety net. In Maura's world energy was gathered and sustained much differently, so it would take the police a while to locate her—but they would. Only a few scientists with top clearance were allowed to time-travel, and then only as observers. No one was allowed to wander in the time stream illegally . . . too dangerous. The cops always caught illegal time swimmers and prosecuted them.

She pushed the recorder button on her watch, and as she walked, she made a private recording to cope with her sense of isolation. Plus, it gave her an opportunity to practice speaking in the odd cadence of the area. "All right . . . I've gotten myself into a situation," she confessed to her recorder. She went on to detail her day and her surroundings. "Maybe I shouldn't have fiddled with the device, but it was just lying there. Who wouldn't have messed with it?"

Guilt struck. She was a thief, which went against her moral grain. But she was also a first-year university student, on track to become a Mind Doctor, and a member of the two percent of her population born with the DNA of a Sensitive. The competition was fierce for the coveted degree and life's work as a Mind Healer. Travel into the past would give her a leg up on her first research paper. And if she did no harm while in the past, maybe the authorities would be lenient with her.

Maura walked to the house where she'd first materialized and hunkered in the bushes, grateful for the clothing that kept her comfortable. Her stomach growled. "Forget it!" she told her hunger. "Nothing I can do about food right now." She tucked the time-travel device into a pouch in her bodysuit, crossed her arms and waited for sleep and for the long night to end, facing the only house where she might go and the only person who knew she was here.

2

Maura watched two cars leave Dylan's driveway, one with a man driving, the other with a woman driving and two young girls in the back. Her heart leapt, hoping that the boy, Dylan, was still in the house. She rang the doorbell, heard someone banging around inside, felt her heart hammering. The door was flung open.

"What did you forget, Luc—" Dylan stopped midsentence, stared out at her. "You!"

Maura smiled weakly. "It's me."

"The girl who ran away from me."

"I—I was scared." She had formed her story during the night between bouts of sleep, part truth, part fabrication. Every lie cost her a jolt of pain in her head. Sensitives had finely honed consciences, and lies sent discomfiting waves through their brains. Now she was starving and had to lie as she stood in the past confronting humans of lesser intelligence.

"Maura, right?" He leaned against the doorjamb. "You weren't jogging yesterday, were you?"

"Hiding in the bushes." The lie made her wince.

"Why?"

"I didn't want them, the police, to find me." Truth.

"The police? Why are the police after you?"

"I ran away." A half-truth. Small jolt.

"From what?"

"A bad situation."

A flicker of empathy showed on his face. As a Sensitive, Maura was able to read others' moods and the auras surrounding their bodies. Dylan's aura was cloudy, meaning he was troubled. "What do you want me to do about it?"

Maura tried to appear pitiful, which was in fact the case—she was in a mess and needed help. "Can I bum some food? I'm really hungry."

His expression softened and he stepped aside. "I can feed you. Kitchen's this way." She followed. He said, "I thought you were my sister, Lucy. She always forgets something and has to come back for it. Mom's taken her and my other sister, Casey—they're twins—to ballet class. Not that they can dance. But they think they can."

Maura appreciated his easy chatter, an attempt to make her feel comfortable. Something she'd said in her partly fabricated story had connected with him.

In the kitchen he directed her to a barstool at a high counter, where she sat, trying not to let her eyes dart everywhere at once. The kitchen was an archive from over a hundred years before her time. She had no idea what some of the equipment was for.

He pulled open the door of a large box that lit up, and rummaged inside. "What would you like?"

Maura was stumped. Her survey in the library had been extensive, but she hadn't zeroed in on food. "Some fruit . . ."

"Come on, you need some real food. How about I fix you some toaster waffles and ham?"

She had no idea what he was offering. "Sounds good." She watched, fascinated while he poked discs into slots in a machine and put a slab of something pinkish into another machine called a microwave. Minutes later, he was pouring liquid goo atop the stack of discs and shoving the plate toward her. The scent was awesome. She tasted the waffles, liked them immediately, but wasn't fond of the ham. She realized ham was meat, and her family didn't eat meat—too expensive.

As she ate he leaned toward her on his elbows from the opposite side of the counter. "Now why don't you tell me what's going on with you."

She stared down at the plate, echoed a story she'd read about a homeless boy in the library. She was also homeless, so she knew her words were believable. "I ran away a while ago. Just been living however I can. I need to hold up, get a job, make some money so I can keep on moving."

"Money's critical to travel," he said.

In her society there was no money, only credits and

debits, but she understood the concept of payment for work performed.

"Why'd you run?"

"Bad home scene." Big jolt. She had the best family in the world. "I-I'd rather not go into details. If that's all right."

"No pressure. Where's your stuff?"

Stuff. What did he mean?

"Your things," he said. "Clothes, bedroll, whatever."

She chewed on her lower lip. "I don't have any stuff."

"You left with nothing?"

"Short notice."

Dylan grinned, shook his head in disbelief. "Didn't you have a plan?"

"No plan."

His expression sobered. "Must have been a really bad situation."

She watched his aura darken. The words *bad situation* had hit some mark inside him, turned him pensive. Nonchalantly she asked, "You ever been in a bad situation?"

She felt him shutting down, pushing her away emotionally. "You could say that."

Maura backed off. The nerve she'd hit with her question had alienated him. "Well, then you understand what's going on with me. I have to hunker down somewhere. Just until I can pay my way out of here."

"I can't put you in our garage like some homeless cat."

"Oh, I'm not asking—"

"It's okay. I get it. Your back's to a wall. You need help."

She nodded, watched him as he considered her problem, turning it into his own. Amazing! This perfect stranger was willing to help her. She'd been taught that people from the past were self-centered and totally devoid of values. He wasn't a Sensitive. He was a male human from the past with noble impulses. Unexpected.

"My dad's a vet," he said.

She sorted through a jumble of new words in her brain. "An ex-soldier?"

Dylan looked quizzical. "No. An animal doctor. Dad runs a clinic. He usually hires extra help in the summer. Maybe I can put in a word for you."

"That would be good." In her future only the wealthiest people kept pets. "And really nice of you."

"Yeah, I'm such a nice guy."

The nuance of bitterness in his voice took her aback. He was really telling her he *wasn't* a nice guy. She let it pass. "Now, about your garage . . ."

He smiled. "Won't work. But I might have something else for you. I'm cutting grass, doing odd jobs for neighbors this summer. I'm house-sitting for the Carters two blocks over."

"You're sitting in their house all summer?"

He shook his head, looked puzzled. "I'm watching their house while they're gone. Get it? I water their plants, feed their two cats, and keep an eye on the place. If I set you up to live there, you can dump litter boxes every day and feed the beasts. I'll give you twenty-five percent of the money they're paying me."

She'd have to return to the library, get on those slow ancient computers and figure out what he was asking of her. "I'll do it," she said, clueless as to what she was signing on for. Still, how difficult could it be?

"But you can't be seen by the neighbors," Dylan said. "No lights at night. No coming and going out the front door."

"I'll be careful." She was amazed by the lengths he was going to just to help her out. What a research paper she could write. Her classmates were limited to viewing the past through a time prism, watching without hearing conversations, making assumptions based on intuition. Images, but no involvement. Maura had *gone into* the past. She was living it, expanding her knowledge base, which would serve her profession in countless ways. If she got home and wasn't prosecuted. Cheater, her conscience shouted.

"I'll walk you over." Dylan plucked a set of keys off a hook by the door.

"You'd do this for me?"

"Sure. My payback good deed to the universe," he added.

Again she heard a bitter edge in his voice.

Suddenly the kitchen door flew open and two little girls hurtled into the room. They stopped cold when they saw Maura at the counter. Behind them came a short woman juggling purse, clothing and dance shoes. "Dylan I thought you were going to cut—" She too stopped when she saw Maura.

Maura slid off the stool, her heart pounding and her body poised to run.

3

"Hello," Dylan's mother said. "Have we met?"

"I'm Maura."

"Sandra Sorenson."

"She's staying a few blocks over." Dylan said. "With her grandparents for the summer."

His mother smiled, accepting the explanation without hesitation. "Where are you from?"

Maura flipped through maps she'd studied in the library. "Kansas," she said, hoping it was a good answer.

"Like Dorothy," one of the girls said.

Maura didn't know any Dorothy, but she nodded agreeably.

"Butt out, Lucy," Dylan said. "We're not in Oz." He waited a beat, added, "Maura needs a job. Dad hired on for the summer yet?"

"I don't think so," Sandra said. "How old are you, Maura?"

Maura didn't want to admit to being only fifteen. She'd read that people from this time weren't really considered adults until they were eighteen. "Seventeen," she said. "Almost eighteen."

Lucy piped up with, "Me and Casey are eight. Dylan's eighteen. He's older than you."

This surprised Maura. In her society, eighteen-year-olds were either finishing university studies or living in co-ops, working and earning credits toward their futures and the futures of their aged loved ones. Only rarely did an able-bodied person as old as eighteen remain at home. In her day, hard work and planning were required of everyone.

"Girls, go up and change," Sandra said. Both of them bounced out of the kitchen. Sandra turned to Maura. "Are you good with animals? Can you deal with yappy dogs that might bite? Cats that scratch?"

Of course Maura didn't know, but she said she could.

"I'll speak to Jerry tonight. Maybe you can go into his office and meet him and see the place tomorrow."

"Absolutely. Thank you."

Dylan said, "Okay, all set. Come on. I'll show you that place we were talking about."

Maura followed him outside. "You have a nice family."

He shrugged. "I guess."

She knew he was glossing over sentimentality. He liked his family, but something was not right. She sensed it. There was a darkness that separated him from them.

She itched to know more, but she would have to get the information properly. As a Sensitive, she could read thoughts and scan memory cells. As a doctor-in-training, she wasn't allowed such privileges unless a patient was under her care and she had his or her permission. If she was going to be a doctor of the mind and spirit, she mustn't invade and take information. Unguarded thoughts and memories and discards of the mind were fair game, though, akin to overhearing a conversation between strangers.

Maura fell into step beside him. "Where's your father's office?"

"Too far to walk. I'll pick you up around eleven tomorrow and take you. And take you to lunch after. You'll be hungry again by then."

She thought about it. "I guess you're right."

He laughed. "I'll bring over a hamburger and fries tonight, plus some other food."

She thought about the ham he'd fed her this morning. "Vegetables are fine. And fruit."

"You're a vegetarian?"

"Is that bad?"

"No . . . it's just that—I know someone else who is. Once knew someone." He corrected himself.

His aura darkened; his eyes saddened. "Whatever you bring me, I'll eat," Maura said cheerfully. "Doesn't matter."

Two blocks later, he turned onto a walkway leading

to a trim brick house. "Your new home," he said, unlocking the front door. He punched a keypad on a small wall panel. "I'll write down the security code for you." Of course, Maura already knew the code from Dylan's unguarded thoughts. "Use it when you come and go. Punch in the code, go out the back door. You'll have about a minute before the house gets locked down."

Two cats met them inside the front door. Each stopped, tails twitching, and watched Maura. "The beasts?" she asked. The animals' brains weren't complex and she had no trouble making the cats feel at ease.

"I'm impressed. They're usually pretty squirrelly," Dylan said.

She guessed he meant rambunctious. She held them still for a minute with the power of her mind, then released them, and they bounded off.

Dylan walked her through her responsibilities for the cats and the house. The idea of tossing out cat poop seemed wasteful. In her society, nothing was thrown away. All matter, even waste, was recycled, a necessity to keep the earth clean and productive.

Dylan said, "The Carters have a teenage daughter. She's heavier than you, but you might want to borrow some of her clothes until you get paid and can buy your own." He shifted from foot to foot. "I've got to go. You all right until I come over tonight?"

"Sure." She stopped him at the door. "Thanks for your help. Really. I need it."

He shrugged self-consciously. "I need the good karma."

She closed the door, wondering what he'd meant. Except for the cats scratching something with their claws, the house was still and quiet. Maura strolled through her quarters, reveling in the solitude of noncommunal living, likening the house to a museum. If only she could take pictures on her recorder. She didn't dare. The time police might pick up the activity from another time period. She decided to return to the library the next day and zero in on information that would help her win a job and blend in better.

She closed her eyes, revisited her morning with Dylan and his mother, and the tension she had sensed between them, so real she had seen auras of disturbance around them, even around the twins. Dylan and Sandra acted like nothing was wrong, but that was a lie. *Something* was wrong, and it acted like a wedge keeping them apart and at odds.

Maura considered her own duplicity, the half-truths and outright lies she'd told. She realized that the jolts she received for fabrications had lessened in intensity each time she told one. Professor Trevvida had been correct when he'd once told her class, "Each time the conscience is breached by lying, pain caused by creating lies toughens your conscience. Eventually lies come more readily— until there's no pain at all."

The whole class had scoffed at the time, because a

Sensitive with intentions to heal prided herself on honesty. Now Maura knew that Professor Trevvida had been absolutely correct. She felt some remorse, but she could justify her lying: it was necessary for survival. And for learning. Practicing her skills on a real live patient was an adventure too tempting to abandon. She could help this Dylan face his demons. It would be her gift to him for aiding her.

By the time Dylan picked her up the next morning, Maura was a whole lot smarter about the culture and its protocols. She'd dressed in clothing from her benefactor's closet according to what she'd seen in teen fashion magazines—denim and T-shirts. The clothes were large but acceptable. Plus, their roominess meant that she didn't have to wear the horrible breast-holding contraption of this time. Clothes from her era fitted one's physical form exactly and were comfortable. She tucked the time-travel device into a borrowed purse.

"You look nice," Dylan said when she got into his car. "My dad's expecting you. Mom's waiting at his office too."

Maura sensed a warning. It must have been unusual for Sandra to attend such a meeting.

The office of Jerry Sorenson, doctor of veterinary medicine, was overrun with people holding animals on laps or leashes. Dogs barked and cats hissed from within carriers. Yet in spite of the crowd, Maura was ushered quickly into Jerry's inner office. The man was busy, but

Maura gathered that for some reason, she was a priority. Dylan remained in the outer office, but Sandra went in with her.

Jerry explained her duties, mostly cleaning cages and walking pets recovering from surgery. Maura listened politely, although after studying up on veterinary medicine in the library, she could have performed simpler surgeries herself.

"Interested?" Jerry asked after the job description.

"I'd love the job," she said honestly.

"Let me show you the kennel area."

Maura and Sandra followed him. He opened the door to a cacophony of yaps and barks. "Calm down, children," Jerry shouted.

Maura slid into the room, reached out mentally and instantly quieted the caged animals. She realized she liked pets, especially the dogs, which she found affable and friendly and eager to please.

Jerry stood transfixed. "That's the first time that line's ever worked." He looked at Maura. "What do you think?"

"I want the job." She glanced from cage to cage. The dogs sat docilely, panting.

The three of them returned to his office. "Take this paperwork home, fill it out and return it. I'll let you know in a couple of days."

She was grateful that he didn't want her to complete the paperwork immediately—she had no idea how to fill out the information without Dylan's help. She smiled and said, "Thank you." Then she walked out the door, pulling it closed behind her.

The door was still open about an inch when she heard Sandra say quietly, "You *must* hire this girl, Jerry. Don't you see? She's the first person Dylan's shown an interest in for almost two years! He needs her. We can't let her get away."

4

"Mom wants you to come over for Sunday dinner," Dylan said to Maura. They were sitting at the table in her borrowed house filling out the paperwork for his dad's office job. He didn't seem happy about the invitation.

"Should I come?"

"Your call. I have to leave right after we eat."

Her internal radar picked up loads of signals that some wedge was separating him from his family. "A problem?"

"I won't dump on you."

"I don't mind. Do you want to talk about it?" It was a question a Mind Doctor might ask. She was pleased with herself.

"It's not important. Friends don't dump on friends."

He'd called her a friend. Naturally he didn't think of her as a doctor. How could he? Friendship held a high value in her time; it was a rare bond because of the cutthroat drive to succeed at any cost in her society. Maura counted only one friend in her time period—Shalea. "I-it's all right." She tried to regain her composure.

His blue eyes searched hers and she automatically blocked her thoughts from him, just as she would have if she'd been with a fellow Sensitive. Of course, there was no need, she realized. He couldn't read her thoughts. He was primitive, a part of history.

"I like being with you, Maura." Dylan reached over and took her hand and she felt an unexpected tingling. What was *that* about?

She said, "I—I'm a good listener."

He squeezed her hand, making her heartbeat quicken. "Well, I'm not a good talker." He rose from his chair, breaking the spell. "We eat around five. Bring the paperwork when you come over. I'm sure you'll get the job."

When he was gone, she mentally examined the uncharacteristic physical changes that had attacked her body. Sweaty palms. Accelerated heartbeat without exertion. Rapid breathing. She'd never experienced such physical symptoms by simply looking into someone's eyes. She hurried to the nearest mirror and stared at herself. Her cheeks were full of color. As a Sensitive she was used to experiencing others' feelings—that was her gift. But to go through these feelings personally was extraordinary. She wanted to become a Healer, and Healers had to disregard personal feelings and emotions if they were going to identify with others and aid them. She must check her emotions around him. She was in enough trouble already.

On Sunday Maura found a long skirt and a top in the closet that looked dressier than the tee and jeans she'd worn to the interview. She wanted to look pretty, though she had no logical reason. She walked to Dylan's house in dazzling hot sunlight, wondering how people lived without clothing that changed with the climate, and arrived feeling sweaty and wilted.

When Maura knocked, Lucy opened the door and pulled her into the kitchen, where Sandra said, "Welcome. It's almost ready."

"Got that paperwork?" Jerry asked, pouring himself a glass of wine.

"Right here." Maura handed it over and he plopped it on the countertop without so much as looking at it.

Lucy joined Casey, both tearing lettuce into a large bowl. They were quiet, and their muddy dark blue auras were signs of anxiety. Maura sensed that the whole family was on edge, not a good sign.

"Where's Dylan?" Maura asked.

"Getting ready," Lucy volunteered.

Sandra said, "Show Maura her place at the table, girls. Dad and I'll bring in the food."

Maura recognized the rush to change the subject.

"I folded the napkins," Casey said to Maura in the dining room.

"But I put the knives and forks on the table," Lucy said, not to be outdone.

"I'm impressed by both of you," Maura said.

They were all seated when Dylan clattered down the stairs. He ignored everyone except Maura. "Hey," he said to her. He was dressed in slacks and a polo shirt.

Sandra cast an awkward glance at him. "I was thinking you might not go this Sunday. I mean, since we have company and all."

"I go every Sunday. This Sunday's no different."

"But just this one time—"

Maura was an awkward witness to their tug-of-war. The room filled with gray, muddied greens for resentment, deep angry reds. There was nothing she could do with so many different colors clashing. "I don't mind if Dylan leaves," Maura said, hoping to be conciliatory.

"You're a guest," Sandra said, talking to her son through Maura. "We invited you. Dylan shouldn't run off."

"I'm not running off," Dylan said directly to Maura. "I have somewhere I have to go."

Maura searched discarded thoughts but only found confusion. She forced herself into a Zen state.

"You're mother's right," Jerry said, pouring himself another glass of wine. "You should stay here today. How's it going to hurt to miss one Sunday out there?"

Dylan was clearly finished arguing. "It's a long drive."

"Can't you just eat before you go?" Sandra said. Dylan's plate remained empty.

"I'm not hungry."

"Please . . . ," Sandra said.

"No!" Jerry shouted. "Go. Like it's going to make a difference."

Dylan scowled.

Maura was upset. The room went silent as he slammed out of the house.

"Forgive my son's rudeness," Sandra said, tears brimming in her eyes. "A self-imposed obligation, nothing to do with you, Maura."

"That's okay. I didn't take it personally."

Jerry picked up his glass. "Just so that the day isn't a total downer, Maura, you've got the job in the clinic. Start Monday."

She knew he hadn't had time to read her application, but it didn't matter to her; she wanted the job. "That's great. Thank you."

"I'll be in the den. Baseball game on TV," Jerry said.

Sandra stared pensively at the lit candles on the table. "Maura, you and the girls eat. My appetite's gone, but don't let the food go to waste."

Lucy grabbed the bowl of mashed potatoes. Casey hung her head.

"I'm starved," Maura said. Another untruth.

Sandra stood. "Just leave the table when you're finished. I'll clean up later."

"No way," Maura said. She reached out and softened Sandra's sorrow with a few strokes of her thoughts. It was the least she could do.

Sandra said, "You girls help."

Sandra left and Maura and the twins ate dinner in silence until Lucy leaned forward conspiratorially. "They don't like him to go see her."

Casey shushed her. "Don't talk about it."

Lucy shrugged. "So are you Dylan's girlfriend now?"

Maura straightened, watched Casey stir a cold mound of mashed potatoes on her plate aimlessly. Lucy was swinging her legs under the table, making the tablecloth sway in a steady rhythm. Maura chose her words carefully. "I'm a girl and I'm a friend, so, yes, I guess I'm his girlfriend."

Lucy looked exasperated. "I mean a girlfriend like Catherine."

"You better hush," Casey hissed. "I'm telling Mom." She jumped up and ran out of the room.

Lucy ran after her. Both girls were hollering for their mother before they hit the foot of the stairs.

Maura leaned back in the chair, mulling over the revelation. The name Catherine was completely foreign to her. She'd not had an inkling, not a hint about this person before Lucy had divulged it. Who was she? What hold did she have on this family? On Dylan?

*   *   *

Maura liked the job at Jerry's office. The animals were sweet and were always overjoyed to see her. The dogs were happy creatures, easily controlled with her mind. Dogs had short memories and great devotion to their caretakers and owners. Loyal. She liked that trait in them.

She walked to Dylan's house each morning, hitched a ride with Jerry, or with Dylan, if Jerry had left early. She never asked about the disastrous Sunday meal, and Dylan never offered an explanation. She bided her time, hoping she'd have enough of it to be helpful and healing to him.

She liked being near him and was disappointed on the days she missed seeing him. Her favorite evenings were when he came over and they watched television together. She thought the programs terribly boring, but his closeness made her feel cozy, comfortable, and often when his jeans-clad leg brushed her bare skin, she felt the now-familiar tingle she'd originally felt guilty about. Chemical, she decided. Like the effect the presence of humans had on dogs. The physical sensations were purely reactive and therefore totally chemical. She would mention the phenomenon in her research paper if she ever got to write it.

She studied his aura, usually melancholy shades of gray and brown, denoting feelings of worthlessness, but she did notice that when she was with him his aura often morphed into a quiet shade of green calm and peace. That meant he liked being with her. She could read his mood instantly, but kept her self-made promise not to probe his thoughts. She hoped she'd have time to soothe his troubled mind before the authorities found her. She tried not to think about that.

She rarely made a mistake around him, but once, when neither could find the TV remote, she switched the channel with her thoughts. "How'd you do that?" he asked, astounded when the channel jumped unaided to the one he wanted.

Realizing her mistake, she said, "I didn't do anything."

"Who did?" He looked around the room, which held just them and the cats. "Channels don't switch without a remote."

"I did it with the power of my mind. Didn't you know? I'm an alien come to earth to seize control of television viewing."

He grinned good-naturedly, searched her eyes for a long moment. "You're a very different sort of girl, Maura."

Her pulse rate shot up. "Is that bad?"

He leaned forward and kissed her forehead. "Not a bit."

His mouth felt warm on her skin and her heart almost rammed through her chest.

He leaned back, draped both arms on the back of the sofa. "Let's go out. Come on. We'll have fun."

"Let's go," she said scooting off the sofa. She headed for the door, but it took a full minute for her to gain her inner sense of control before they left the house.

5

The night air was heavy with the scent of summer flowers, and Maura loved the soft sweet aroma that reminded her of her mother's garden. As she rode in Dylan's car he fiddled with the radio, seeking music he liked. She didn't care about the music. She only knew how happy she felt being with him. She wondered if this was common in the past, this driving along roads and feeling contented. In her world, she'd be studying, working to get ahead of other university students. Kids had little leisure time, and if she had any, she'd visit her family home before returning to the university co-op where she lived full-time with two roommates.

"What are you thinking about?" Dylan asked.

"Contentment. I like it."

"Far cry from your former life, huh?"

She recalled the story she'd told him about running

away. He believed the half-truth and she wanted him to keep on believing it. "Yes, thanks to you."

A frown crossed his face, and a shadow, his mind. He didn't like compliments. For reasons unclear to her, he didn't think himself worthy of kindness or praise. "I'm glad you're happy."

She could have asked him why he wasn't content, but didn't. She hoped he'd reveal his secrets willingly. She wanted him to trust her enough to tell her what his mind was hiding. "Where are we going?"

"First stop, ice cream," he said.

"Real ice cream?"

"Is there another kind?"

She'd eaten ice cream once at the birthday party of a wealthy classmate when she was twelve. Dairy products weren't plentiful in her society. Most dairy—milk, cheese, ice cream—was made from plants like soybeans, easier to digest and cheaper to grow and manufacture. "What's your favorite flavor?"

"Rocky Road."

"Sounds yummy," she said, with no idea what it was.

The ice cream store was in a small cluster of buildings next to a movie theater. Inside, the lights were garishly bright, but the place smelled heavenly. Confronted with buckets of ice cream inside refrigeration cases, Maura just tagged after Dylan and chose what he did. He bought them both heaping scoops in large waffle cones. Maura's mouth watered and she decided that perhaps the past wasn't so backward after all.

They were sitting at a small table eating when the door swung open and a cluster of laughing kids pushed into the store. "Great movie," one guy said.

"Stupid movie," a girl countered. "How many cars were destroyed making that flick?"

Suddenly one of the boys looked over at Dylan and Maura. "Hey! Dylan! Is that you?"

Maura detected a change in Dylan instantly. He'd grown anxious. His green aura darkened.

The boy came over. "Hey, bro. How're you doing, man? Haven't seen you since school let out."

"Hanging," Dylan said.

"How's—uh, you know."

Dylan's mind hunkered down and went protective. Maura saw a section of his brain sealed off by unscalable inner walls, with sentry cells guarding the perimeter. She realized that the walls had been there all along, but for some reason this boy's appearance had allowed her to see them clearly.

"The same," he said. "Nothing's changed."

The other boy's gaze cut to Maura. "Who's this?"

"A visitor," she interjected. "Dylan's just showing me around."

Another boy at the ice cream cases called, "Brad, what flavor do you want?"

Brad's eyes searched Dylan's face. "It's good to see you, man. Glad you're getting out."

Maura heard a note of pity in Brad's words.

"If you ever want to do something—"

"Yeah. Sure," Dylan said, cutting him off. When Brad rejoined his friends, Dylan tossed what was left of his cone into the trash. "Let's blow," he said to Maura.

She tossed her cone away too and hurried outside after him. In spite of the night, she saw that his aura was a chalky charcoal gray, almost black.

When the car was rolling, she asked, "Don't you like Brad?"

"He's all right."

She sensed a sea of pain swelling inside of him, went silent, knowing instinctively that it was what he needed. Brad had triggered despair in Dylan, and he'd retreated deep into himself, leaving her out in the dark.

Dylan took a side road off the main drag and then another road that was more like a bumpy trail leading out to the countryside. He stopped at a place with an empty field on one side and a row of trees on the other. The stretch of trees ran along a river. Dylan turned off the engine and opened his car door. "Come on. I'll show you one of my favorite places."

Maura fell into step beside him. The trail stretched ahead like a white ribbon under a full moon so brilliant that a halo glowed around it. A million stars studded the night sky. Gurgling water splashing over stones reminded her of mellow, resonant bells.

He cut through the tree line, and in the moonlight, she saw that the ground dipped and flattened into rocks smoothed by an eternity of flowing waters. Beyond the scattering of stones, the water ran slower, and midstream, the water lay still. On the far bank stood another line of trees guarding the shoreline. "This spot by the river is one of my favorite places in the whole world," Dylan said.

The sounds of water, tree frogs and night insects were all around them. In the future, all rivers were off-limits to people, and could only be accessed with a special license and an escort. Some families were on a waiting list for years for the privilege of vacationing and fishing on a riverfront. She envied Dylan's freedom.

Dylan bent, picked up a smooth stone, held it sideways and sent it sailing across the water. The stone skimmed the surface, hitting, then jumping four times before sinking.

The trick fascinated her. "How did you do that?"

"Haven't you ever skipped a rock?"

"No. Why do you do it?"

He grinned, picked up another rock and repeated the feat. "For fun. To see how many times I can make it bounce before it sinks."

Defying gravity. She liked the idea. "What's your record?"

"Seven. Here, you try it." He picked up several stones from the clear water. "You need flat ones. You hold it sideways and fling." He demonstrated and the rock bounced three times.

Maura took one of the stones he offered, tried to imitate his sideways toss. Her stone plunked into the water. He showed her again how to hold and throw one and she tried several more times without success. She growled at her lack of skill. He made it look so easy, and she wasn't used to failing at anything.

"Wait," he said with a laugh. "Let me help." He loaded up on flat stones, stepped behind her. He put his left arm around her waist, pulled her against him. He ran his hand down her right arm, placed the back of her hand in his palm and said, "Pull back like this."

All reason, all logical thought fled her brain. Her nerves quivered. Her breath went tight in her chest as his warm breath hit the nape of her neck. "There's a rhythm to the throw." His soft words fell like flower petals against her ear. "Don't concentrate too hard. Feel the stone; let your fingers curve around its edges." He limbered her arm, bringing it back and forth, still helping her grip the rock. "Success is all in the wrist. Easy."

Maura felt one with him, not the stone. She wanted to melt into his skin, soak into his body, swim inside his veins.

"Now," he said.

The stone flew sideways from her hand and skipped three times over the water before sinking. She might have been satisfied if the moon hadn't been shining so brightly, if Dylan hadn't had his arms wrapped around her. She had no defenses for what she was feeling. She wanted to press herself into his body, to place her mouth on his, to taste him, to savor him as she had the ice cream.

He turned her to face him, touched her face. He touched his forehead to hers. She joined their minds, summoned all she was feeling and poured it into him, let his feelings come into her. His mind held raw hot desire. *Desire, an uncommon longing that can consume body, mind and will.* The definition hit her hard, remembered from a text-book, an early primer for Sensitives. Sensitives were to be masters of their emotions, not victims.

She was supposed to be his doctor, and he, her patient. She had almost crossed a forbidden line. "I . . . can't . . ." Trembling, she slipped from his arms. Cold seeped through her although the night was humid and muggy. He had wanted her and she had wanted him in ways that frightened her. A physical coming together, a sexual union between them would not be right.

He took several minutes to regain control of his breathing. A clear, bright red aura engulfed him, signaling sexual arousal. "My bad," he whispered, stepping away.

"I'm sorry," she said, meaning it in a thousand ways he would never understand.

"I just haven't felt that way about anyone for so long," he confessed in a halting voice.

How could she tell him she'd *never* felt that way? Nor was she sure she'd ever feel that way again. She took his hands in hers and said, "Please, tell me about Catherine."

6

Dylan was startled. "Lucy?"

"Lucy," Maura confirmed. "That Sunday dinner together. She talked about Catherine being your girlfriend."

Dylan stared across the river, searching for a way to begin, while Maura waited. He needed time, and she needed to shelve what had almost happened between them.

"Catherine Buckley was in my sixth-grade class. We hit it off. She was a tomboy, a good athlete, liked insects and frogs and all kinds of animals. We'd catch tadpoles together, put them in a fishbowl, watch them turn into frogs and let them go. We were best friends, and by ninth grade, I started to notice she was a girl." Dylan smiled. "Some of the guys started ragging on me about her. It didn't matter. I really liked her. We just slipped into boyfriend-girlfriend mode and hung together all the time."

Dylan's memories were unguarded, free flowing, and

Maura watched images fan out like a photo display, like a movie, even the pictures that wounded her. Pictures of Dylan and Catherine as children, then of them kissing and exploring one another's bodies, of them lying tangled in each other's arms naked, and of them sometimes stealing an hour of sleep only to wake, dress and part.

In her time, males and females were separated at age ten into same-sex groups. Male-female pairings were arranged according to DNA compatibility, dictated by scientific standards rather than random chance. In the dorms, late at night, schoolgirls whispered in the dark about which boy they would be assigned. Maura had not yet been paired, but had wondered what her partner would be like, and whether she'd care for him. Two of her friends had been assigned a mate—one was happy about the selection; the other, not so much. Love for your selected mate was a wonderful happenstance, a luxury, not a requirement.

She asked, "Did you love each other?"

"We thought we did." He halted. His thoughts became a jumble, and Maura sensed a feeling of disloyalty haunting him. "Yes," he said emphatically, to banish the feeling. "I loved her."

"But something happened to her," Maura said, urging him to continue his story.

"We were in a car wreck."

"What happened?"

He rubbed his forehead. "I'm not sure. We were

coming home from a party. I woke up on the ground outside the car. Catherine was slumped inside. She was unconscious. I was hurt."

Maura watched the scene from his memory's perspective—the hard-packed earth, the view of the car window, Catherine half-slung out the window, smoke coming from the front of the crushed hood. Maura winced as the physical pain from Dylan's accident hit her. Sensitives were allowed to absorb patients' hurts as their own for the sake of identifying with them, and to relieve some of their anguish.

"My leg was broken in three places. Two broken ribs. Blood in my eyes." His pain crossed from the physical into mental. "I saw smoke and knew the car might blow up. I crawled to the car, somehow got her out and far enough away so that when the car exploded, she wasn't burned."

The scene was horrific to Maura—she'd never seen a car accident. In her time, special chips were embedded under road surfaces and into vehicles. The chips, not drivers, controlled traffic. "Were you burned?" she asked, already knowing he had been because she felt hot pain along her left arm.

"On my arm."

"Seems to me you were a hero. Pulling her out of the car and all."

His eyes narrowed and his memory clouded, cutting off the flow of images. "I'm no hero."

Maura saw the walled-off section of his memory loom

like opaque glass. She couldn't see through it, wasn't sure he could see through it, either. Often the psyche built barriers to seal off very bad memories. Dylan's mind had built such a wall. As a doctor, it was her job to help him tear it down and deal with what lay behind it. If she was given enough time, she was certain she could heal him.

Cut off and unable to see his memories, she asked, "Did you save her?"

Dylan worked a stone from the riverbed with the toe of his sneaker, bent, picked it up, took his time to answer. "Would you like to come with me Sunday afternoon and see for yourself?"

"You'd let me come with you?"

"If you like."

He might be taking her to a cemetery. "I would like to go with you."

He slung the stone, watched it skip five times over the water's surface. "I'll pick you up at two."

Someone was watching her house. Maura felt traces of a presence the second she went in the door. The cats, which always mewed and greeted her when she arrived, had hidden under the bed. She discovered them quickly with her mind probe. Her senses tingled and she tasted real fear. The time police were the only entities who could have come. They hadn't yet breeched the security system or the mental safety block she'd set up around the house's perimeter. But eventually they would.

The next day, she went to Jerry. "May I take one of the abandoned dogs home with me?"

Jerry kept a few animals, fed and cared for them, worked to find them good homes. "What's up?" Dylan's father asked.

She put on a worried-scared expression that wasn't entirely fake. "I thought I heard prowlers around my house last night."

"Where are your grandparents?"

She remembered she was supposed to be staying with them. "They're sort of deaf."

Jerry nodded. "Sure. Take Chowder."

The big German shepherd could be difficult, but Maura was one of a few who could handle him. "Thanks. I'll bring him back once I feel safe."

"Maybe your grandparents will want to keep him," Jerry said hopefully.

"Maybe," she said, hating to lie again but knowing it was necessary. Chowder was accustomed to cats, and Maura personally found that cats were good company, requiring little care. But the dog would bark if he sensed anything unusual near the house. He would warn her if she was in danger from the searching probes of the time cops, and she would have time to run.

On Sunday Maura dressed in clothes she'd bought with her paychecks, adding big sunglasses to hide her eyes and avoid broadcasting any telltale messages about her feelings for Dylan and the possibility of seeing Catherine's grave. Now knowing he was suffering from survivor's guilt—the guilt people felt because they lived though another had died—she would be able to treat him more easily. Yet whatever was lurking behind his memory's walls remained a mystery.

He picked her up promptly at two o'clock. They talked little, or rather, Dylan talked little. Maura told stories about Chowder, how he had jumped up on the kitchen counter and gobbled down the frozen bagel Maura was getting ready to toast for her breakfast. "The bread was frozen solid, but he got it down in about three chews and a swallow."

Her story drew a half smile from Dylan, yet the farther he drove into the country, the less she was able to engage him. His aura was charcoal rimmed in black, the color speaking of death and unforgivingness. At one point she braced for him to turn the car into a cemetery they were approaching, but he didn't turn. He kept driving down the long straight back road to his destination. Maura waited, repressing her ability to read his thoughts. She vowed to be patient, to let him take her to whatever it was he so dreaded. When he did turn, it was to enter a long driveway with a low brick building at its end. A sign read GOOD SAMARITAN REHABILITATION CENTER.

Puzzled, Maura followed him through sliding glass doors to a lobby, where a woman was sitting behind a reception desk. She looked up, smiled. "Hello, Dylan. Good to see you."

"Here to visit," he said. "A friend," he added, motioning to Maura.

The woman eyed Maura. "Both of you need to sign in."

They complied; then the woman buzzed them through another set of glass doors. Dylan walked down a hall with sure steps, obviously knowing his way well. Maura kept pace. He stopped in front of a closed door and rapped softly. "I come on Sunday afternoons because no one else is usually here," he explained. "I don't like other people around when I visit."

Maura's heart was pounding; she was positive that what lay beyond the door was at the root of Dylan's unstoppable pain.

Though she heard no summons to enter, Dylan eased open the door and she followed. There was a single bed in the room, plus a dresser and a bedside table. In the bed lay the frail, thin body of a girl with a ventilator hose snaking out of her throat.

"This is Catherine," Dylan said, a catch in his voice. "She's in a persistent vegetative state. So tell me, Maura . . . is she dead or alive?"

7

Maura slowly raised her sunglasses to see Catherine more clearly. The girl's body was a husk, yet her nails were groomed, lovingly manicured and painted, her dark hair brushed and held away from her face by a sparkly barrette. Her eyes were open but expressionless.

Catherine's life force was missing. Her mind, her essence, no longer remained. The hallways of her thoughts and experiences were empty, the landscape gray and dead, like earth scorched by a nuclear blast. Maura saw nothing but a wasteland of tangled nerves and blood vessels and vacated memory cells. All that was functioning were the girl's automatic reflexes. Her heart beat; her lungs filled only with an assist from the ventilator. Her eyes did not see; her ears could not hear.

Dylan walked to the bed, bent and kissed Catherine's forehead. "Hi, baby," he said.

His words stabbed Maura's heart.

"She blinks," Dylan said. "She wakes and sleeps. She can move her arms and legs. She even smiles. But it doesn't count. It's reflexive. That's what her doctor tells us—me and her parents, her sister. She's here but gone. Crazy, huh?"

Maura had read about PVS in textbooks, but she'd never seen such a patient. It was so sad she wanted to cry. "I—I'm sorry. . . ."

"Everyone's sorry. Except Catherine. She doesn't know a thing." Dylan stuck his hands in his pockets. "So now you see why I'm no hero? Why did I save her? For what? For this? The accident happened two years ago, July fifth. We were at a party at Brad's folks' house on Mirror Lake."

Maura had familiarized herself with the Clarksville area in the library and brought up a map inside her head. The lake was a smudge of blue on the north end of the city. And she remembered Brad from the ice cream store. Maura saw the image of the house and lake that Dylan projected.

Dylan rocked on his heels. "She was in a coma at first. That's when we all had hope that she'd wake up. But she didn't wake up."

"If they pulled the vent—"

"They did. She kept breathing without it. So they put it back to make it easier for her."

Maura examined the shunt inserted directly into Catherine's abdomen to supply water and liquid food.

She stood transfixed, overcome with pity. "Without the feeding tube—"

"She'll starve to death." Dylan's words conveyed sheer hopelessness. "Her parents won't allow it."

Maura knew Dylan couldn't face that consequence either. Dylan, Catherine's family, her doctors and caretakers, couldn't "see" inside the girl's brain as Maura could. They used tests and machines to confirm what Maura's Sensitive abilities viewed plainly: no amount of care was ever going to bring Catherine back. She was a living corpse.

"So you come every week to visit her," she said.

"Of course. It's because of me that she's here."

"How do you figure that?"

He rubbed his forehead. "I was driving. I braked to keep from hitting a deer that jumped out into the road. The car skidded. I woke up on the ground. That's all I remember."

Most of his story was true, but Maura realized parts were conjecture manufactured by logic, reconstructions of the few memories he did have. But the glass wall in his mind was still intact. She ached to know what lay behind it, and fought the temptation to find out. "I should wait outside," she said, stepping back toward the door. "You came all this way to visit her. Take your time."

He turned to the bed, picked up Catherine's limp hand and kissed it. Maura couldn't bear to watch. She left the room, steeling herself, wondering how she was going to help him when, despite all her intellectual abilities and willpower, she was falling in love with him.

In her dream, Maura's two worlds were colliding. Her future time stream kept blending with the time stream she lived in now. She saw her parents in Dylan's house; her mother, Diane, working over Sandra's old-fashioned cooktop. Her mother's image brought pangs of loss. She missed her, and wondered how her family felt about their daughter's being a time fugitive. Picking up the time-travel device and recklessly pushing the button had changed everything about her old life—not only for her, but for the people she'd left behind.

Still, if she hadn't pushed the button, she'd never have met Dylan or tested her clinical skills. Be truthful, she told herself in the dream. Her interest in Dylan far exceeded her medical interest in him.

She saw her best friend, Shalea, sitting on the sofa in the house where Maura now lived. Maura ran to her. "I've missed you so much!"

"We've missed you too," Shalea said, her manner offhand, as if Maura had been gone fifteen minutes instead of almost three months. Shalea was reading, studying the piece of glowing electronic paper in her hands. "You've missed so many classes. How will you catch up?"

Maura waved away her friend's concerns. "Let me

show you whom I've met." As a Sensitive, she could place pictures into others' minds, and she did so, focusing her efforts on the moonlit night by the river. She sent every sensation she'd felt too: the shivers, the pounding heart, the feel of Dylan's skin, the scent of him and the night air.

"Wow," Shalea said. Her dreamscape eyes grew wide enough for Maura to see her own reflection in the pupils. "What do you think you're feeling?"

"Love."

Shalea burst out laughing. "That's silly. He's an antique. He's no better than a caveman. You can't love him. Aren't you curious about whom the elders have paired you with? A modern man, for sure."

Maura began to cry because Shalea's words hurt her. "Not true. It's wonderful to discover someone you love by chance. Much better than some guy assigned by committee. Besides, Dylan needs me."

"The committee is protecting your DNA, making sure it goes to offspring who will shape society."

"You sound like a professor. Think with your heart, Shalea."

The scene shifted and Maura was in a dark wood. She heard wolves growling, saw their red eyes glowing in the night. Her heart seized, but when she turned to run, her feet were rooted to the ground. The growling intensified. She panicked, felt a scream rise in her throat.

She woke with a start, heard real growls next to her

ear. Chowder. Maura bolted upright in bed, listened carefully. "What's wrong, boy? What do you hear?"

The dog's simple brain was easy to navigate. She heard what Chowder was hearing, twigs snapping in the yard, caught the scent of "stranger." Maura's heart hammered. Whatever was outside hadn't penetrated her mind shield yet. If it was the authorities though, it was only a matter of time before they did.

Days later, Jerry had an emergency case come into the clinic. Sandra came to pick up Maura and run her home since Jerry couldn't and Dylan had a job that was running late. As Maura got into the car, she said, "Thanks a bunch. I didn't want to wait around. No telling how long the emergency will last."

In truth, Maura wanted to be home at night. She felt certain that when the cops came for her, they'd come at night because it would be easier to take her under cover of darkness. She wanted a chance to escape when they came, and she wanted to feel herself close to Dylan and the area they'd met for as long as possible.

"No problem," Sandra said. "I had to take the girls to dance recital practice. The big event is Friday night, with a nice reception afterward. I hope you'll come."

"Wouldn't miss it."

"Hey, why don't you come by the house and have dinner with me? I fed the girls earlier, but I haven't eaten. Nothing fancy, just a burger."

"I should get home."

"Dylan can run you home. He shouldn't be too much longer."

The thought of seeing Dylan broke Maura's resolve. Eating something she didn't have to cook was appealing too. Unfortunately she'd developed a taste for meat, especially hamburgers with melted cheese.

"I've been hoping to get to know you better," Sandra said.

Maura sensed a hidden agenda but wasn't offended. She had many questions for Sandra as well. "Can't pass up a good meal," Maura said brightly.

In Sandra's kitchen Maura watched the woman slap raw meat into flat patties. Maura hated the look of the meat, but once it began to cook outside on the grill, the aroma made her mouth water. While Sandra tended the burgers, Maura sat at the patio table and poured herself a glass of iced tea from a frosty glass pitcher.

"Have you had a good summer? Anxious to go home?"

Maura realized Sandra was softening her up for the real questions she wanted to ask. Maura saved her the trouble by saying, "I went to the rehab center last Sunday with Dylan, and I saw Catherine."

Sandra's expression went from cheerful to haggard.

Maura said, "Dylan told me about the accident. He told me everything." She wanted to build Sandra's confidence, wanted Sandra to know it was safe to talk about the tragedy with her.

"Did he, now?" Sandra said skeptically. "Everything, you say."

"Um—everything he said he remembered," Maura said, confused and less sure of herself.

Sandra turned from the grill to face Maura. "Did he also tell you that he tried to kill himself because of it?"

8

Maura felt blindsided. After all the time she'd spent with Dylan, how could she have missed it? Was that what he was protecting behind the wall inside his head, the actions of grief, guarded by sentries of memory cells? "No," Maura said. "He didn't tell me."

Sandra slumped, her expression turning raw. "He was hurt really badly himself in the accident. In the hospital, in traction after surgery, his leg set with steel rods and screws. He couldn't even visit Catherine, and when he did . . ." She paused. "At first, she was in this coma and we kept thinking, 'She'll wake up any day now.' But she never did. She just sank lower, and nothing the doctors did made a hill of beans' worth of difference."

Maura sensed Sandra's despair, but she didn't interrupt the flow of her story.

"The longer Catherine lay in the hospital, the deeper

Dylan went into depression. His body healed, but his heart—" She looked out to the perfectly maintained back-yard, the well-trimmed grass, the freshly mulched flower beds.

Dylan's work, Maura realized. Ordered and groomed and expertly kept. The work that held him together.

Sandra said, "He missed months of school. He had to repeat his junior year. We got him tutors so he could fin-ish with his class, but it made him angry. 'I'll finish when Catherine docs,' he told us.

"'But she'll never finish,' his dad and I told him. 'You have to go on with your life.' Instead, last summer he tried to *take* his life."

Maura shuddered. Tears welled in her eyes. Suicide, a Mind Doctor's greatest failure. "What did he do?"

"Went in the garage and turned on his car after clos-ing and locking all the doors. I'd taken the twins shop-ping and Jerry was at the clinic. We'd replaced the car that was burned in the wreck. At the time, we thought it would cheer him up. Can you imagine? Cheering up clin-ical depression. We were stupid."

Maura knew that wasn't true. Dylan just hadn't been diagnosed. "You shouldn't blame yourselves. . . ." Maura's stock answer embarrassed even her. "I—I mean, that's what I've heard."

Sandra shrugged. "Thank God Lucy got a stomachache and we had to leave the mall early. When I opened the garage door, the exhaust fumes and carbon monoxide almost knocked me over. I called nine-one-one and he was rushed to the hospital. They saved him, and we made certain he went into therapy."

Maura saw the scene in Sandra's head like a three-dimensional movie, the garage full of toxic fumes, the twins screaming hysterically, Sandra pulling an unconscious Dylan from the car and out onto the driveway. "Did the therapy help?"

"It seems to. He takes medicine, visits his psychiatrist, though not as much as he used to. He returned to school last spring and will face his senior year this fall."

"But he still insists on seeing Catherine once a week," Maura said.

"Yes. It breaks our hearts, but he won't give it up."

Penance, Maura surmised; a way to soothe his guilt. "Do her parents blame him?"

"I don't think so. It was an accident . . . every mother's greatest fear. Dylan and Catherine were sixteen. Their curfews were midnight, and when our phone rang at one a.m., I knew something horrible had happened."

Maura thought of her own mother. Was she mourning the loss of her daughter?

"We rushed to the hospital, fearing the worst. Dylan was conscious, and Catherine's parents were so grateful she was alive. . . ." Sandra paused. "Now they maintain her at the rehab center even though there's no hope."

Sandra gave Maura a wondering look. "Do you know that the longest record for survival of a PVS patient is over forty years?"

In Maura's time, there were no PVS patients. Once Medical Sensitives proclaimed a human being dead, food and water were withdrawn and the victim died. To her, prolonging such a patient's life seemed primitive and a poor practice of medicine. "I didn't know."

"You've been good for him, you know."

"Me?"

Sandra smiled. "Yes, you. He's been happier these past couple of months than in the last two years."

The words pleased Maura, but the feeling of satisfaction was brief.

Sandra sighed. "We'll miss you when you leave. I wish you lived closer. I wish you went to school here. But I guess your parents miss you terribly."

For the first time in a long while, Maura felt a jolt from her conscience, remembering the lies she'd told Dylan to explain her sudden appearance in his time stream. Without his help, she would never have been able to stay. And she never would have had the experiences that had enriched her life. She would have never had fallen in love. True to his word, he'd kept her secrets—lies all, but Dylan didn't know that. "I hate the idea of leaving too," she said with more sincerity than Sandra could possibly understand.

Sandra pulled the burgers off the grill, but they looked shrunken, black and hard. She stared at them. "I ruined the burgers. Let me go make some more patties."

"That's all right," Maura said, standing once she saw how dark it had grown. "I've got stuff at home to eat, and you probably have to leave soon to get the girls, don't you?"

"Oh my gosh! I let the time slip."

"No problem."

Sandra thrust a bag of chips at Maura. "I've got to run. I can drop you at your grandparents' on the way."

"I like walking. It's only a couple of blocks."

"Help yourself to anything in the kitchen," Sandra said, hurrying into the house for her purse and car keys.

Maura waited on the patio until she heard Sandra's car leave the driveway, feeling sad, adrift in time, and lonely. She missed her family, wished she could figure out what to do. She couldn't stay, and she would be in colossal trouble if she returned. But what choice did she have? Better to return voluntarily than to be jerked home by the cops. She picked some vegetables from Sandra's small garden and walked around to the front.

Bright headlights nailed her as she tried to cross the driveway. Her heart skipped a beat. Dylan's car stopped and she calmed down. "Hey," she called.

He got out of the car, came up to her. "Chips and veggies for me?"

"If you want them." Just the sight of him made her pulse race and brightened her mood.

"No . . . I'm trying to quit."

She weighed his words, realized he was joking. "Me too." Stars had begun to pop out overhead. "You finished for the day?"

"I'm finished." He looked bone tired.

"I was just going home. Want me to stay awhile?"

"Um—about that. The Carters called today. They'll be home Friday, so that means you'll have to vacate."

"In two days?" Tension gripped Maura.

"I know it's short notice. Look, if you want, you can crash here for a few days. Until you're ready to go home. Or run again. You should have some money saved up by now. Wasn't that your plan?"

That was what she'd told him. "How would I explain it to your family? They think I'm at my grandparents. What reason could I give for leaving their home for yours?"

He thought about it, rubbed his temples. "We'll come up with something tomorrow."

"Sure, we'll figure something out," she said, knowing she was out of options. She had to go.

Dylan draped his forearms over her shoulders, lowered his forehead to touch hers. His skin was still warm from his day in the sun. She closed her eyes, breathed in the scent of him, stored the puff of his breath in her memory cells so that whenever she needed to, or wanted to, she could conjure him up, could bask in the feel, scent, taste of him. She envied the past Catherine had with him, the sweetness of it. She imagined that he loved her, Maura, as he'd loved Catherine.

He raised her chin a fraction of an inch and brushed his lips across hers. This time she didn't stop him. "We'll think of something," he said, and pulled away.

Maura fought tears, turned abruptly and jogged down the sidewalk, her heart aching. And yet, as she ran, it struck her that in spite of what Sandra had told her earlier, Maura had sensed no antidepression medications in Dylan's system. None at all.

9

Maura cleaned the house, erasing all traces of her long stay. She had total recall, so it was simple to restore each room to its original state. She even turned coffee-table books to the exact angle arranged by the Carters. The cats watched from atop an armoire, their tails twitching with interest and curiosity. "You are nosey beasts," Maura told them, very glad that animals couldn't talk. "But I'll miss you."

Chowder was much more concerned about her activity, and he was anxious and unsettled. The dog followed her from room to room, staying close to her heels, sometimes making her trip over him. She often stopped working, trying to reassure him. She would miss him, and understood why owning a pet was so popular in this day and time. They brought comfort and affection and were of great service to the elderly and lonely. Too bad keeping one was prohibitively expensive in her time.

She sat on the sofa and Chowder rested his head on her knee, staring up at her with sad brown eyes. Maura rubbed his thick fur, scratched behind his ears the way he liked. She cupped his muzzle. "Don't worry. I'll make sure you get back to Doc Jerry. He'll find you a good home."

A lump rose in her throat. "Thanks for taking care of me. They would have found me sooner if you hadn't warned me." Chowder tilted his head. "I'm going back," she told the dog. "Better to go on my own than with the cops, don't you think?" She gazed into the dog's questioning eyes. "Maybe I can explain how I only wanted to help Dylan. I was making headway too." She would still be punished, though. She disliked imagining that part, but facing punishment was mandatory. "I'm not *changing* anything," she reminded the dog. Maybe it would count in her favor when she stood in front of the judge for sentencing. The penalties for time travel without permission were harsh, but changing history was the ultimate crime.

Tomorrow she'd drop her clothing, plus everything else she'd acquired in this time stream, into a charity bin. The money would be an especially nice discovery for the organization.. She planned to take the dog to Dylan's house on Friday evening while everyone was at the dance recital. She'd told Jerry at work that day that her grandparents would be bringing her to the recital.

Jerry had grinned. "Good! We've wanted to meet them."

Leaving Dylan would be the hardest of all. Best to

never see him again. "Eventually people here will forget about me. So will you." She ruffled Chowder's fur. "Someday Sandra or Jerry or the girls might ask, 'Whatever became of that girl who just vanished one night?' And Dylan might say, 'She was a runaway. Probably didn't want to go home.'" Once he filled in details, they would have an acceptable explanation for her disappearing act and they would forget she ever existed.

But she would never forget them.

On Friday morning she fed and watered the cats, took all her personal belongings to the charity drop and went to Dylan's house, where she hitched a ride to work— her final day—with Jerry. The day seemed to move more swiftly than usual—an impossibility, of course. Time moved the same way every day, second by second, minute by minute, hour by hour. She told each animal goodbye. Most understood. They absorbed human emotions, and mourned when they cared for a person who was troubled in any way.

After work she rode with Jerry to his house. Dylan's car was gone, which made her both sad and glad. Acting nonchalant with him when she knew she was leaving would be difficult.

She got out of the car. Jerry called, "See you at the recital."

"Sure thing."

At the Carter house Chowder greeted her from the

backyard, where Maura kept him during the day. She brought him inside, fed and watered him, washed the bowls and put them away in the cupboards. She greeted the cats, who acted aloof. They were distancing themselves from her, uncanny in their ability to convey their displeasure. "Don't be snooty," she told them, but they turned tail and stalked from the room.

Maura changed into her jumpsuit, felt the material mold to her skin. She hadn't put it on in months, and it felt strange. Chowder bounced around her feet. "Cool it," she told him. He ignored her command.

She looked around, was satisfied with the way the house looked. No trace of her. The Carters would never know she'd lived there. She sat on the sofa, lamps off, the time-travel device in her hand, waiting for darkness to fall. The recital would be in full swing. She imagined Lucy and Casey twirling on the stage and smiled. As a Sensitive, Maura's whole life had focused on education, on honing her gift for the greater good of society. It might have been fun to take dance lessons.

Suddenly she bolted upright. Chowder went tense beside her. Something was wrong in the universe. Her nerve endings tingled and her brain cells snapped. Dylan! Her spirit closed the distance between their houses and connected with him. He was in trouble. He hadn't gone to the recital. He was at home and in pain. Maybe the cops had traced her to his house. She'd never put security around his house! "Stupid!" she said. Maura had to get to him. She hurriedly snapped the leash onto Chowder, set the alarm system and zipped out the back door. Once outside, she ran.

She arrived at the house out of breath. Chowder, alert and on edge, panted and strained against his leash. The house's windows were dark. No . . . there was a faint flickering light from Dylan's room. She connected with his mind and was saddened by the blackness of his aura. She thought about banging on his front door but knew he wouldn't unlock it. She remembered where Jerry hid the extra key and went for it. Inside she let Chowder off his leash, forced the dog to stay put with the power of her thoughts and took the stairs two at a time.

She opened Dylan's bedroom door cautiously, eased inside. Dylan was sitting cross-legged on the floor, a candle burning in front of him. An empty wine bottle lay on the floor. Another half-empty bottle stood beside him. He was shirtless, and sweat glistened on his skin. He held a large hunting knife over the candle, its blade glittering in the light. Her heart almost stopped. "What are you doing, Dylan?"

He glanced up, flashed a half smile. "Maura. What are you doing here?"

His pupils were dilated. His body swayed to the movement of the flame like some ancient warrior facing a great challenge. "I thought I'd to go to the recital with you," she said.

His brow furrowed. "I'm not going."

"What did you tell your parents?"

"That I was working."

"Lucy will be mad at you if you miss her big night."

"Lucy will get over it." His words were slurred. He twisted the knife over the flame.

She fought to stay calm, wrest control from him. "Put that down, Dylan."

"Why? See how shiny it is?" He twisted the handle, making the candlelight glimmer on the silver blade.

Maura inched closer, taking small steps so as not to alarm him. "Knives are dangerous."

"I'm counting on that," he said, and with a single motion he flicked the tip of the blade across the flesh of his inner arm. A fine line of blood oozed from the superficial slice.

"Dylan, stop!"

"Why?"

"I—I care about you. I . . . don't want you to be hurt."

He looked up, as if seeing Maura for the first time. "Catherine died today. Her heart quit."

His words were like stones hitting her. "Oh . . ."

"Her mother called me. She was crying, said it was better this way." He stared at the candle's flame. "Better to let her body join her spirit."

"She was already dead, you know."

"My fault."

Maura knelt on the floor in front of the candle. "Hurting yourself won't bring her back."

His unfocused eyes rose to meet hers. "It'll make me feel better." He picked up the half-empty bottle and took a drink, made a face. "Burns." He tried to set the bottle upright on the carpet, but it tipped and fell. The red liquid spilled across the beige carpet like blood. "My fault," he said. "I killed her."

Suddenly Chowder went crazy barking at the foot of the stairs. Maura sucked in her breath. The police had found her. She had probably led them here. Once they found the room, they would seize her and wipe Dylan's mind. The mind wipe would be thorough, perhaps enough to damage him, turn his mind mushy. They would leave no trace of her.

Maura could wait no longer. She eased into his mind, saw the glass wall of protection guarding his memory and struck it hard. The wall began to crack. She watched the crack widen, fall in jagged shards, scatter across the landscape of his memory. He dropped the knife, grabbed his head. In that instant they both saw clearly what he'd been hiding from everyone, even himself.

She reached out to steady him as he swayed with pain and self-loathing. *His fault.*

His eyes widened, incredulous. "Are you in my head? I can feel you, see you. You're inside my head!"

Chowder's barking went insane. The animal would give her the few precious minutes she needed; Maura was fairly certain the cops from her time had never faced down an angry dog. She released Chowder, gave him a single command. *Defend!*

Dylan clamped his hands over his ears, scrambled backward on the carpet, his face contorted with fear. "Who are you?"

Pinning him with her mind, she said, "I'm the person who's going to save you."

She snatched the time device from her waistband, set the destination and pressed the button.

10

She materialized into a stand of trees at night, alone.
Lake water lapped at a nearby shoreline. Humid heat
immediately soaked her face and trembling hands. She
saw the lighted house on the edge of the water in the distance. It matched the image Dylan had given her the Sunday afternoon they'd gone to see Catherine together.

Maura set out to find Dylan. Music grew louder as she
approached the house. Deafening. The front door stood
wide open. Couples, clinging to one another or clustered
in groups, lined the hallway inside. The main room over-
flowed with kids, most of them very young and drunk.
They shouted above the roar of the music while their bodies writhed to the beat. Cigarette smoke barely masked
the smell of beer. Nearby, a girl shrieked when a boy put
an ice cube down her back.

Maura searched the house with a mind probe to locate Dylan. He wasn't there. She turned to go back outside,

ran smack into the chest of a large, well-muscled boy. "Hello," he said, taking her by the shoulders.

She pushed him into a wall with the sheer force of her mind. "Have you seen Dylan Sorenson?"

He banged into the wall, rubbed his left shoulder. "Whoa! What's up with you? Did you just shove me?"

She stared him down, determined that he had no knowledge of Dylan's whereabouts and walked out the front door, gulping in fresh air. She had to find Dylan quickly. The cops were stranded in the future for now, but they wouldn't stay there for long. Away from the house, Maura saw cars and pickup trucks, more abandoned than parked. She hurried to the field, looked for Dylan's car, the one that she'd only seen in the vision of the crash. Blue. Yes, it had been blue.

It was dark among the cars, but she heard raised voices and went toward the sound. She saw an interior light shining from an open car door, and then saw Dylan and Catherine standing beside the door. Her heart did a stutter step. She'd almost arrived too late.

Dylan at sixteen looked heavier, certainly more self-assured than the boy she'd met at eighteen. Catherine also looked far different from the wasted girl Maura had seen on the bed in the rehab center. She was tall, with thick dark hair hanging past her shoulders. And she was very pretty.

"Give me the keys, Dylan." Catherine sounded exasperated, as if they'd been arguing with one another.

"Aw, come on, baby. I'm fine."

"No. You're not fine. Let me drive."

"Nobody drives my fine machine but me. Them's the rules."

"You drank too much. You're not thinking straight."

Dylan said, "How many fingers am I holding up?" He thought the comment funny and laughed uproariously.

Catherine stamped her foot. "I want the keys."

He held the keys over her head. She jumped for them, but they remained just out of reach.

Maura had seen the truth inside Dylan's mind back in his bedroom and knew how the argument had originally ended. Now was the time to intercede. She walked into the scene. "Hi."

Dylan and Catherine looked startled. "Private party," Dylan said, annoyed.

"Why are you shouting at each other?"

"Who're you—the party police?" Dylan demanded. "Get lost."

Maura's heart twisted. Of course, he'd never seen her before. They were strangers in this time stream. "Just passing by, heard the yelling. Just checking it out."

"Well, just keep on passing," he said, with an elaborate bow from the waist.

Maura glanced sideways at Catherine, who was standing with her hands on her hips looking frustrated. "The keys, Dylan."

Laughing, he said, "Catch if you can." He tossed them

high in the air and Maura took a deep breath and did what she'd come to do. She committed a time traveler's worst crime. She pushed Dylan aside and let Catherine catch the keys. He cursed at Maura, staggered backward, tripped and landed hard on the ground.

With one motion, she had changed history.

Dylan had been driving the night of the accident. He'd swerved to miss an imaginary deer and lost control of the car, crashed and burned. And Catherine had died.

"Ha," Catherine said triumphantly, gripping the keys tightly. "My keys now." She ran around to the driver's side, opened the door, slid in and started the engine before Dylan could get off the ground. He came up shouting at Maura.

Maura ignored him. "You're okay to drive, aren't you?" Maura asked Catherine through the open passenger door.

"No booze for me. Taking cold medicine. If I touched a single drop, Mom promised to ground me forever."

Dylan staggered next to her and Maura grabbed his arm. "You're not too steady, buddy."

He shook his head, tried to remember why he'd been shouting at her, but the beer had fogged his brain. "It's my car," he mumbled.

"Will you help him get in?" Catherine asked.

"I can get in by myself," Dylan growled, his angry outburst forgotten. He didn't resist when Maura pushed him into the passenger's seat.

"Thanks for your help," Catherine said. "I thought he was going to win this fight."

"I'm glad he didn't," Maura said. She reached across Dylan, grabbed the seat belt and pulled it, locking it into the slot, securing him. As she straightened, she turned her head to look him full in the face.

Dylan's eyes focused. His brow furrowed. "Don't I know you? It seems like I do."

"No," Maura said. "You've never met me."

She shut the door and Catherine maneuvered carefully out of the space, steering around several parked cars.

Maura watched until the taillights became red pinpricks in the distance. She slumped against a tree, her legs rubbery, adrenaline gone. Now what? She couldn't go home. She couldn't stay here. Once the authorities discovered what she'd done, they'd follow her with a vengeance. But she also knew that Dylan, the boy she had known and loved, was safe and that Catherine was alive.

Maura realized she had only one way to go. "I'm a Healer," she told the night sky. This was her life's purpose, the mission of her DNA. She could be a Healer in any time stream. As long as she held the device, she could keep moving, crossing through time forever, until they caught her or she died. She liked freedom. She had worked, met and cared about people and animals, strangers all. And she had tasted love. She liked the flavor.

The chemistry, the roller-coaster emotions, the sheer ecstasy of pure chance had been magical.

She held up the time-travel device and randomly reset numbers. What did it matter where she landed? She pushed the button and vanished.

Lurlene McDaniel began writing inspirational novels about teenagers facing life-altering situations when her son was diagnosed with juvenile diabetes. "I saw firsthand how chronic illness affects every aspect of a person's life," she has said. "I want kids to know that while people don't get to choose what life gives to them, they do get to choose how they respond."

Lurlene McDaniel's novels are hard-hitting and realistic, but also leave readers with inspiration and hope. Her books have received acclaim from readers, teachers, parents, and reviewers. Her bestselling novels include *Don't Die, My Love; Till Death Do Us Part; Hit and Run; Telling Christina Goodbye; True Love: Three Novels;* and *The End of Forever.*

Lurlene McDaniel lives in Chattanooga, Tennessee.